FALLING

Book 2 of the FADE Series™

By

Kailin Gow

FALLING: FADE Book 2

Published by The EDGE Books from Sparklesoup Inc.

First Published 2011

Copyright © 2011 by Kailin Gow

Published by theEDGEbooks.com.

For information, please contact:

Sparklesoup Inc.

14252 Culver Drive, #A732

Irvine, CA 92604

First Edition

Printed in the United States of America

ISBN: 978-1597486170

Henceforth space by itself, and time by itself, are doomed to fade away into mere shadows, and only a kind of union of the two will preserve an independent reality. – Hermann Minkowski

ONE

My name is Celestra Caine. Celestra. Caine. I will not forget that, no matter how much people want me to. I will not.

Memory is all we really have. All we are. Without memories to give us a context for what's happening around us, anything could be happening. Without the memory of my name to cling onto like a life preserver in a sea of insanity, I could be anyone. Anyone they want me to be. Given all the craziness that has taken place within the last few weeks, knowing my name is vital. I won't let it go.

I'm Celestra Caine.

Celestra Caine, the seventeen year old senior at Richmond High. Celestra Caine, who used to train for track with her boyfriend, Grayson, and studied hard in the hopes of making it into Georgetown on a scholarship.

Celestra Caine, who had normal friends, and a normal family. A normal life. I'm her.

The trouble is, I'm so much more than that as well. I am, for example, the girl who came back from practice one day to find her family gone. Just gone, like they had never existed. The girl who picked up the phone in the family living room to hear the message that changed my life.

"Celestra Caine? You are about to fade."

Such simple words to change a life. To make me into a whole different person. Celeste Channing. That's who I'm meant to be. The daughter of a tycoon, playing at being a model, partying. It's so far from me that I can barely believe it, but then, I guess that was kind of the point.

And it isn't all bad. I *like* being glamorous. I *like* getting to live the rich life, and I really like getting to spend it with Celeste Channing's suave boyfriend, Jack Simple. Though the name is ironic, because there is never anything simple about Jack. He's Celeste Channing's boyfriend. If I'm still Celestra Caine, then is he really my boyfriend too?

When it comes to boyfriends, it's hard not to think of Grayson. When I was still Celestra Caine, we were so close. We were going to go to the same university together. We were going to spend the rest of our lives together. We would spend our time studying, or running, or just hanging out. It was enough just to be around him sometimes, knowing that he was everything in the world to me and I was everything to him. But that was before I stopped being Celestra. That was before I was 'faded'.

No. I'm still her. I won't let that go. Not even when it would be so much more straightforward with Jack if I did. But then, it wouldn't solve everything. He's complicated. We're complicated. Jack is every girl's dream. He's handsome. He's suave. He's dangerous, but he can keep me safe. Literally, given that he's a secret agent charged with keeping me alive. He's everything I could want. Certainly everything Celeste Channing could want.

But I'm not her. I'm not sure who I am anymore. Not after everything I found out from the people Jack works with. I'm not human. I'm not even close to it. I'm faster, stronger, more dangerous. I can burn people alive with a touch. Celestra Caine couldn't do that. Nor could Celeste Channing. Jack's mother could, but that's another story. Maybe it's one of the reasons I like him. Or maybe it's even more complicated than that.

I know that there are people, the Others, who want to eliminate me. I know that there are other people, the Underground, who want to save me. Or at least study me. What I don't know any more is what direction my life is going to take. How can I? I don't know if I'm a freak, or a schoolgirl, or an international model. I don't know if tomorrow is going to feature black clad assassins trying to kill me, secret bases full of stored memories, or powers I have no idea how to control.

I don't even know who to love anymore. Grayson, the love of Celestra Caine's life, who might have been playing a role my whole life just to get close to me? Jack, the current flame of Celeste Channing's life, who has spilled over into so much more than that, going beyond the parameters of his job to love what he has seen of the real me? Both of them? Neither of them?

I don't know. They say that the truth is important. That we should treasure it. But sometimes, I have to wonder if it would be better if I had never learned it. My life, Celestra's life, used to be simple. Everything is complicated now that I know the truth, and there's no sign of it getting better any time soon. I fell down the rabbit hole, and the more I try to scramble for the sides, the faster I fall.

I won't give into it though. I won't let the chaos of my life in the last few weeks crush me. I won't let it change me, even though I'm still not sure who the real me is. I *will* get my life back. Sooner or later, it will happen, and when it does, I will be ready for it. No matter how much the Others and the Underground try to pull me away from it. No matter how much Jack and Grayson pull me apart without meaning to.

I will be ready. I will be everyone I need to be, and I will not let it destroy what's left of my memory. I will understand everything that is happening to me, deal with all the things that are threatening to kill me, and make all the people I care about remember who I am. I will do it, and until I do, whatever happens, I will cling tightly to the thought that has kept me sane this far:

I am Celestra Caine.

TWO

How did I get into this position? How did I get into a spot where I'm standing outside a secret base, with my ex-boyfriend pointing a gun at his own father while the boyfriend who has become so much more than his cover identity demanded runs towards us, ready for battle? How did I get to the point where I'm stuck between two secretive organizations, neither one of which will let me go back to my life as Celestra Caine?

I don't know, and I don't have time to think about it. Even as Jack runs forward with the other Faders from the Underground, Grayson glances around at them, and his father, Richard, starts forward as though he might take the gun from him. Grayson barely steps back in time.

"Grayson," he demands, "what are you doing? Aim that gun somewhere else, right now!"

Grayson's aim doesn't waver, which isn't like the boy I grew up with. But then, I don't know how much of that boy is left. Somewhere along the line he has been reprogrammed; taught things far beyond how to run track and keep me company.

"Sorry, Dad," he says. "I can't let you get Celes. She's not what you think she is."

Richard looks disgusted at that, glancing from him to me. "I knew I made a mistake when I let you get too close to her."

"That's just it, Dad. You shouldn't have done it in the first place." That sounds more like the Grayson I knew. The one who helped me study for tests and kissed me underneath the bleachers at school. All this confident, well trained stuff is like a veneer over it.

Richard doesn't sound any more normal though. "Son, she's dangerous. She killed two of our men, and she'll kill more before she's done. She'll kill you, too."

"She-"

I hadn't noticed Richard shuffle forward again, but now his hands snap out, taking the gun from Grayson in one smooth motion. Does everyone around me have advanced training these days? Though as he points the gun straight at me, I know that's the least of my worries.

"Dad, don't!" Grayson moves between us; in front of me. It puts him right in his father's firing line, so that if

Richard wants to shoot, he'll have to shoot his son first. That seems like a huge gamble to me, because nothing I've seen suggests that the Others care about that kind of thing. But then, maybe I'm just thinking about the way the Others forced me to move away from my own family for their safety, and about the way they hounded Jack's non-human mother.

Richard doesn't shoot, but he does look furious with Grayson. "You know how pathetic you sound, you lovelorn puppy? Remember, she broke your heart, ran away with some guy from the Underground. You don't even know if she ever loved you or if she was just using you."

I know they didn't complete the process of Fading Grayson's memories, because he broke clear of the room before they could, yet he looks blank at that. It's like he doesn't remember anything about us having to be apart, or about the way Jack broke up with him on my behalf by text. Grayson's so stunned by that he takes a step to the side. Not much of one, and obviously not deliberately, but it's still a step. I brace myself for the shot.

It doesn't come, because Jack and his team have arrived. Jack tackles Richard low, grabbing him around the knees and bearing him to the ground, where they wrestle for the gun in a tangle of limbs. For a moment, I find myself wondering why Jack didn't just shoot the other man, but I squash that thought. I can imagine how much pain it would cause Grayson, seeing his father killed.

Even as Jack wrestles with Richard, his team are fighting with the Others. Some fight hand to hand, following the example of their leader. Others exchange gunfire with them, using the surrounding cars for cover. The Faders from the Underground have the advantage of surprise, but it's hard to tell for sure who is winning. There is simply too much chaos.

From that chaos, Jack emerges, kicking Richard's pistol away and drawing his own as he stands. He turns towards me.

"Celes, get back inside. This is no place for a civilian now. And take Grayson. I'll deal with things here."

I don't want to leave Jack like that. He might not be the boyfriend I left behind, but he has grown to be just as close to me, starting off as merely the boyfriend of my cover identity, Celeste Channing, but quickly becoming far more, until the real me loved him as much as the fake one.

Grayson seems just as reluctant, but for very different reasons. He looks down at his father. "Call your men off," he demands. "Call them off, or Jack here will shoot you where you are."

Richard looks at his son with contempt then. "No."

Jack seems to be expecting that, moving closer, the gun pointed straight at the Others' lead scientist. He's going to do it. He's actually going to murder someone in cold blood. And right then, with so many of Richard's friends trying to kill me, I can't bring myself to say anything to stop him.

Then Jack brings the pistol up and down sharply, knocking Grayson's father sprawling into unconsciousness. He turns and fires a couple of shots at the remaining others, helping his fellow Faders to pin them down, before looking over at Grayson.

"You shouldn't try to negotiate. Kill them or don't kill them, but don't talk to them."

"He's my Dad," Grayson says, and again, he sounds more like just the boy from my home town than whatever he has become thanks to the Faders' memory device.

"You thought he'd pull out his men?" Jack ducks below the level of the car as a burst of automatic fire

- 13 -

comes our way, and I do the same. He stands to deliver another couple of pistol shots by way of retaliation. "He'd die before doing that. You're lucky I just knocked him unconscious. At least this way he isn't in the firing line. Now, I'm sure I told you two to get going. Get back to Sebastian."

I notice that Sebastian isn't 'Dad' to Jack out here. This is business, not family, and Jack is his ever calm, ever dangerous self through it. Grayson doesn't look anywhere near as comfortable, and for a moment I think that it is just the violence going on around him, but that isn't it. It's only as he opens his mouth to thank Jack that I get it. He doesn't like owing Jack like that.

"Tha-"

One of the Others bursts around the car, grabbing Jack in a rear choke, while ripping the gun from Jack's hands. The arm that isn't around Jack's neck comes up around the back of his neck, putting extra pressure into the choke. Not that the black clad attacker needs it. He's huge, muscles showing in bunches under the unrelieved darkness of his sweater.

Jack drives an elbow back. It does nothing, while the other man is stuck to him too closely for Jack to get most other forms of strike in. Even when Jack throws himself forward, obviously hoping to drop to his knees and throw the bigger man over the top, nothing happens. The man strangling him is so large, so strong, that he can just hold Jack up while he chokes him.

Grayson starts to grab for the gun, but I don't think that's a good idea. I don't know if he'll be able to pull the trigger, and even if he does, how do I know he won't miss accidentally and shoot Jack?

How do I know he won't miss deliberately?

There's no time to think about it. Jack is already starting to lose consciousness, and I know what I need to do. I step forward, take the big man's arms in mine, and tear them away from Jack. I hear bone break as I do it, but I don't care. Right then, it simply doesn't matter to me. Even when the big man cries out in pain, it doesn't make any difference.

The big man tries to kick me, even injured as he is, and I toss him to the ground. That's when I feel it inside me. The same furious force that let me kill two men out on the road back near my old home. The same power that let me burn them up completely when they chased me and

Grayson after I had broken the rules by going home to see him once more.

The big man seems to sense it, because he tries to crawl away. I don't let him. It's far too late for that. He tried to hurt Jack. Tried to hurt one of the people I love. I reach out for him, snatching him up like he doesn't weigh twice what I do. He hangs for a moment in front of me, out at arm's length.

Then the power rushes into him.

I'm not aware of sending it into him, but I don't try to stop it either as it pours out of me like raw sunlight, burning its way into the man and then burning back out of him white hot as it shines from his eyes, his mouth. It glows like a furnace, and it burns as hot as one. So hot that the man who tried to hurt Jack can't scream. So hot that I shouldn't be able to touch him. I stand there, and I burn him, until I'm holding nothing but a human cinder, then I drop him to the ground, looking around with my eyes glowing brightly.

It's then that I managed to regain some control. I push down the part of me that's looking around with that feral, energy filled gaze, trying to find the next person who represents a threat. I push it down even though it seems to burn through my blood as I do so, squashing it, compressing it, locking it away. I push it down until I can look out again and know that I am in complete control. Though what scares me is the thought that really, I always was.

I look down at the remains of the man I have just killed, feeling the horror of it start to seep into me, the way it did with the two men I burned before. I want to throw up, or run away, but I do neither. I force myself to stand there and get a grip instead. It's only then that I realize how quiet it is.

There should be shots. There should be the sounds of people fighting, shouting orders to one another or crying out for help. There should be the crash of people falling against cars and the dull pings of bullets ricocheting off them. Instead, there's nothing. It's only when I steel myself to look around that I see why.

They're staring at me. All of the Others. All of the Faders. They're staring at me like they don't know what to think. Like they've just seen what I really am for the first time. Even Jack and Grayson are staring, though for them, it's with worry, not horror. Not much horror, anyway. They have seen what I am before. I look around at the rest of them, and they flinch back, like they're all asking the same question. The same one I'm asking quietly, in the privacy of my head.

What happens now?

THREE

The silence seems to go on forever, with the Others and the Underground's Faders just staring at me. Everyone is quiet. Everyone is still. It feels a little like the moment before the gun sounds in a track meet, and I can't help remembering all the ones I've been to with Grayson. That feels like a lifetime ago now though. *Two* lifetimes ago, in fact, because there's my life as Celeste Channing in the way.

There's one point of movement now, and I look around to see Sebastian Cook walking towards me from the Underground's base. He doesn't look frightened, the way so many of the others do. Instead, he looks rapt, as though what I have just done is something he has been waiting his whole life for. Then again, he probably has. After all, I know from Jack's memories as they played on the walls of the Underground's viewing room that Sebastian wasn't there when Jack's mother used the same kind of energy on an attacker. He has spent his whole life trying to understand those like me, and now he has finally seen one of us in action.

I hope it was worth it.

The Others and the Underground seem to shake themselves then, and shots start to ring out once more. I dive for cover behind the car again. Grayson is already waiting for me, while Jack is a couple of cars away, crouched behind one of the Others' Jeeps. They keep their heads down as bullets fly, and Jack returns fire blindly now. Grayson seems to have concerns beyond the fight though as he looks from me to Jack.

"What happened?"

"You know what happened, Grayson," I say. I don't want to think about what I've just done. Sadly though, it seems that Grayson does.

"Why is it that every time Jack is in trouble, your powers come out?"

"I don't know." Actually, I think I might, but I don't want to hurt Grayson's feelings like that. There are some things he won't want to hear.

Unfortunately, he's a good guesser. "Maybe it's because you care a lot for him, Celes."

"I don't know," I say again. I don't know what else *to* say. Grayson doesn't want to hear how much I care about Jack. He doesn't want to hear every detail of the weeks we spent together when I was pretending to be the tycoon's daughter, Celeste Channing. He certainly doesn't want to hear how the kisses and close moments designed to convince the world that Jack and I were a couple in love gradually became real, until neither one of us knew how to untangle ourselves from the closeness we'd created.

"It's because you love him," Grayson insists, and he doesn't sound angry. Just sad. So very, very sad.

The truth is that's probably only part of it. A big part of it, admittedly, but not the whole truth. Jack is at least partly what I am. His mother was the same as me, and I'm sure that connection is part of what makes the fire I can use burn. Through love... yes, it probably is down to that too. After all, the two times I've used my powers have been moments of incredibly strong emotions, and what emotion is stronger than love?

Jack stands, looking like he's going to make his way over to me. He doesn't get a chance though, because in that moment, the large hangar that serves as a front for the Underground's base blossoms into fire, an explosion ripping through it. The blast is not just deafening, it's palpable. The shock wave of it knocks everyone who was standing from their feet. Jack, the Others, everyone. In the silence that follows, part of the Underground's building collapses inwards, flames licking at its framework.

People start to struggle to their feet, but I see that Sebastian Cook isn't one of them. He was closer to the explosion than almost anyone, and he's down on the ground, unmoving. Jack races over to him, heedless of the potential for getting shot, and I find myself doing the same. We need to get him clear of the base, because there's no way of knowing if there will be more explosions or not.

Sebastian rolls onto his back as we approach. "It's a good distraction, don't you think?"

That's one way of putting it.

"Plus it stops what we have to leave behind from falling into the wrong hands. Oh, don't worry. We moved your family's memories out before we blew it up."

I hadn't even thought of that, but I sigh in relief to hear it as Sebastian struggles to his feet. He doesn't seem to be moving very well. And there are bigger problems.

Over by the cars, I see Grayson's father start to stir. He looks at me standing next to Sebastian, and he points.

"What are you waiting for? Get her!"

Most of them seem a little reluctant, but one of the black clad mob of Others is quicker than the rest, and he grabs for me. I half expect to feel the same power as before rising up to incinerate him as his hands close on me, but nothing happens. I'm left trying to fight him off with nothing more than my ordinary strength, and I simply don't know enough about protecting myself for it to work. I try to hit him, and he blocks the blow. I try to wrestle free of his grip and it's solid.

At least it is until Jack gets there. Jack hits the man once, twice, and he falls back, then Jack raises his pistol and shoots him without so much as a warning. Jack tosses me his gun, and then takes one from the belt of the man he has just killed, firing with that uncanny calmness and accuracy he seems to have. I try to join in too, but this isn't the same as facing down an irate trucker, the way I had to when Jack was first taking me to the Underground. This isn't a test designed to see how willing I would be to pull the trigger. This is real.

Real, and chaotic. There are bullets flying everywhere now. Grayson has recovered the pistol he threatened his father with, and is shooting blind. Jack is firing back at the Others precisely, neatly. I... I try to help. I try to stand and shoot back, but it seems like every time I poke my head around the car I'm taking cover behind, I have to jerk it back as a dozen of the Others target me. This is the kind of full blown battle that needs special training, and I simply don't have it.

Of course, Grayson shouldn't have it either. What did they do to him in that memory fading room before he escaped?

Jack swears, and I know that can't be a good sign. "They're getting the better position," he says to me, throwing himself into a roll so that he can end up next to me. A spray of bullets follows his movement. "Pretty soon, they'll be in a position to catch us in a cross fire, and then we're done for, Celes."

I shake my head. "No, there has to be something we can do."

"There is," Jack says, looking at his father. Sebastian nods.

"She's the priority," Sebastian says, and then whispers something to his son.

"What?" I ask. "What are you planning?"

Jack reaches into his inside pocket, pulling out his phone while continuing to send occasional shots over the car one handed. He punches in a number. "Are you in the air? Good. What's your ETA? I know that. We'll have two to pick up. Be ready."

"Jack," I demand, "what do you have planned?"

"There's a helicopter inbound," Jack says. "It will take you to a safe place." He looks at Grayson. "My father says you have received a partial Fade, and that you have also been imprinted with some of the knowledge required of Faders."

Grayson doesn't look certain. "I-"

"If that's true, you're too dangerous to allow to fall into the Others' hands."

For a moment, I think Jack means he's going to have to kill Grayson, and I start to panic. Jack can't do something like that. He just can't. Jack obviously catches my expression, because he shakes his head sharply.

"That means you're going to have to get on the helicopter with Celes. You know where Location Two is?"

Grayson hesitates a moment, then nods.

"Then get Celes there safely. I'm trusting you, Grayson."

"Jack?" I ask.

"I want you to be safe. I won't chance your safety at all. Go with Grayson. He knows where to go."

"And you?" I ask. "What about you, Jack?"

Jack shrugs. "There's only two places on the helicopter. I'll be fine, Celes."

Fine. In a situation Jack has already described as hopeless. He's lying, and I know it, but there isn't time to argue because Jack is on his feet again, shooting one of the Others who tries to get too close. The man falls back, wounded but not dead, taking cover behind another of the cars.

"Why aren't you stopping them?" Richard demands of his troops. A couple more rush forward and Diana, the Fader who was so eager to come out and fight, cuts them down with a burst from her submachine gun before throwing what looks a lot like a grenade. It sails over the Others to explode behind them. I keep my head down. It's gone from being a fight to something out of a war movie in the space of a few seconds.

At least it fits with the helicopter. That's a dull, matt black as it whirs its way in closer. It's not big. As Jack says, there will be barely enough room for Grayson and me. It circles the area once, then picks out a spot between us and the now destroyed base on which to land.

Jack kisses me, fiercely and briefly. "I'll see you again, I promise. Now you need to *run*, because they won't be able to touch down properly."

I don't want to run. I don't want to leave Jack to whatever is going to happen next. Grayson, however, grabs my arm and half drags me to the waiting vehicle, which is hovering inches above the ground with the rotors running fully. He shoves me inside and closes the door after us.

"Fly," he says.

The pilot doesn't need any more encouragement than that. We head up, and I'm forced to watch from above as the rest of the action starts to unfold. I see the others spreading out around the remaining Faders. I see Diana fall, shot by one of the Others. I see Jack unload the remainder of his pistol's magazine, then toss it aside as a couple of the others get close, covering him with rifles. One strikes him in the stomach with the butt of his, and I wince. We barely made it out, and I know I should feel relieved, but all I can think about in that moment is Jack.

Grayson seems to be thinking more clearly. He turns to the pilot, takes a headset so that he can speak over the sound of the rotors, and relays Jack's instructions about our destination. It seems that were going to this Location Two, wherever it is.

FOUR

I look down from the helicopter, and I know we have to go back. Jack's in trouble, with several of the Others attacking him now, beating him while their friends cover him with rifles. They'll kill him like that. They'll kill him, and up here, there's nothing I can do about it. We need to go back.

"Turn the helicopter around," I say to the pilot, but he either doesn't hear me over the noise of the rotors, or he isn't listening. I grab a headset. "Turn it around!"

"Take us to Location Two," Grayson insists, and then rattles off a string of numbers that sound like a latitude and longitude. The pilot nods.

"Turn it around!" I insist, looking down, Jack is on the ground now, barely moving. He's almost too small to see from up here. In another second or two, he'll be gone. I can't allow that to happen. I just can't. I reach forward, trying to grab the pilot. Trying to force him to listen to me.

"Hey! You'll make us crash!"

"Then do what I tell you to," I say, shaking him. "Help me to get back there."

The helicopter lurches violently, and I guess it's only the skill of the pilot that keeps it in the air at all. That doesn't stop me from trying to get him to listen, because I'm frantic now, trying to climb over the seats. Trying to take charge.

Grayson pulls me back. "Celes, you'll kill us."

I rip free of his grip. "I don't care. We have to go back, Grayson."

"We *can't* go back," he insists. "The Others are all back there. It's too dangerous."

"Then I'll kill them. Turn this thing around, Grayson. We have to help Jack."

If Grayson looks hurt by that, I'm not in a position to care right then. Besides, he manages to stay largely calm, even though I can't. "Jack doesn't want us to go back, Celes. He's the one who sent us away."

"And he said he would be fine," I counter. "He isn't fine. He's going to get killed, or don't you care about that?"

"He cares about whether *you* get killed," Grayson shoots back. "You're the important one here. You have to be kept safe, whatever the cost. Don't make Jack's…"

"Don't say it! *Don't* say 'sacrifice'. He isn't dead. I won't let him be dead. I'll kill them all before I let them do that."

"And what about what they'll do to you?" Grayson asks. "They have guns, Celes. They can shoot you before you even get close to them. This is probably the one thing Jack and I agree on. You have to stay out of danger, even if it means other people get hurt. Even if it means Jack gets hurt."

I shake my head. I won't accept that. I won't just fly away and leave Jack to his fate. We'll go back, and we'll collect him, and everything will be all right. Even as I think it, I know I'm not thinking straight, but I can't help it. I make another lunge for the pilot, and again, the helicopter jerks.

"You need to do something about her, or we'll all die," he says to Grayson, as Grayson pulls me back.

"Like what?"

"There's a kit under the seat."

I don't know what he means until Grayson scrambles under the seat, coming out with a wicked looking hypodermic needle, filled with a substance I don't know enough about chemistry to identify.

"Please, Celes," he says, "don't make me use this."

Right then, I don't care. All I can think about is turning the helicopter around. I make a final grab for the pilot, and I feel something sharp press into my arm. I just have time to look around at Grayson accusingly before I slide into blissful oblivion.

Memories come to me drip by drip, inching their way into my consciousness and playing out as dreams as whatever substance Grayson has used to sedate me runs its course. The memories aren't like the ones I saw at the Underground. They aren't of me or those around me exhibiting special powers, or fighting the Others, or anything like that. Instead, they're normal things, simple things. Though that only makes them more painful.

Jack and I are at a party. I don't know which one. There were so many in my weeks as Celeste Channing. We're dancing, and my head is on his shoulder as the music slows. There are people watching us, and I tell myself I'm doing it for their benefit, but now that I can look back on it, I know that I'm not. I'm doing it because I want to. Because I want to be that close to Jack, to take in the scent of him and feel the hardness of his muscles pressed against me.

Now Jack and I are driving. Just driving, for mile after mile. It's just after he has taken me from his apartment, heading for the Underground. He isn't saying much, and I spend a lot of my time sleeping, but now, I can see the concerned glances across at me, the protective looks. I can remember how comfortable it was, taking that long road trip with a man who was, at that point, a stranger to me.

We're in the truck stop, where Jack arranged the test for me. I'm pointing a gun at an irate trucker, one who has been hurting Jack. He takes a step forward, and I pull the trigger without event thinking about it. I remember how proud Jack was afterwards. How confident that he could protect me if I followed his instructions.

Not all the memories are of Jack. Grayson's there too. I remember being in the library with him one time after everyone at school had gone home. Just him and me, with the librarian away somewhere shelving books. We're trying to study for a test, but we can't stop ourselves from talking, and laughing, and kissing.

Now we're on the running track. There are so many memories there, but I know this one well. It's just after I've come back from an injury, and I've been worried about whether I'll be able to run as fast again. Grayson runs alongside me, encouraging me the whole way, and I'm almost a second inside my personal best. Afterwards, we have dinner at my house to celebrate, with my whole family around, just enjoying the moment.

The memories start to mingle now, so that Jack and Grayson follow one another in rapid succession. There's a memory of Jack in the penthouse apartment I had as Celeste Channing, followed by one of Grayson walking with me to school. There's one of Jack firing back as the Others invaded the Underground safe house I first went to, followed by one of Grayson pulling a gun on his own father for my sake. Jack is showing me the memories of the only other person like me beside his mother, then Grayson is running with me to the helicopter. Jack is...

It's going too fast. The memories are swirling now so that I can't keep up with them. Jack and Grayson's features begin to blur into one another, until I realize that

I'm thinking about a club Jack accompanied me to, but I'm thinking about Grayson dancing with me. Their features stretch, and distort, and finally start to spin, in a way that reminds me of something. Something about where I am and what I'm doing...

"Celes. Celes, wake up, we're almost there."

My eyes flutter open, and I see rotor blades spinning above me. Grayson is beside me, looking at me with a mixture of concern and more general nervousness. It's as I remember what he did that the second emotion makes sense.

"You drugged me," I say.

Grayson doesn't look even remotely happy. "I had to. You were going to kill us all if you crashed the helicopter."

The helicopter. I look around, and although we're definitely in a helicopter, it doesn't look like the same one as before. That one was stripped down, military in tone, and clearly built for speed. The one we're in at the moment is very different. It's clearly more about luxury.

"What happened?" I ask. "Are we still near the base? What about Jack?"

I don't care if this helicopter is a different one to the one we were in before, we can still turn it around to save Jack just as easily.

Grayson shakes his head. "It's too late to think about him, Celes. You've been unconscious for hours."

"Hours?" That one word feels like a hammer blow. If it has been hours, then it is too late. Far too late. Jack is... no, I won't believe that he's dead. I won't. Not even when the certainty of it is pressing down on me like a lead weight. He'll have found a way to survive. He has to.

Though I can't think how he could have.

"Where are we?" I demand. "How could you just drag me away like that, Grayson?"

"I did it to keep you safe."

I don't want to have that argument again. Instead, I look out of the window of the helicopter, trying to get some sense of our location. The desert is gone. Instead, we seem to be travelling over countryside, interspersed with small villages and networks of twisting roads. It seems very... different, somehow.

"Where are we?" I ask again. I have to know.

"You know how you've always wanted to go on vacation to England?" Grayson says, and I look at him.

"You're not serious."

He nods. "We took a plane out here, then transferred to another helicopter for the last leg of the journey."

"And you got an unconscious girl through customs?" I ask.

The pilot answers that one. "We have access to private airfields, ma'am. Please prepare yourself for landing; we will be at the specified coordinates soon."

I look down, and I can't see anything like the base the Underground has out in the desert. What I can see is some kind of private estate, with a manor house in the middle of it. It looks kind of quaint and old fashioned, except that as we get lower, I see that there are a whole bunch of aerials and satellite dishes on the roof, hidden out of sight of casual view.

Looking around, I can see that the manor house's gardens are huge. From this high up, I can spot the small town nearby, but there are rows of trees in the way so that the whole place has a cut off look to it. There are outbuildings arranged around the main wings of the house, and I wonder if they will hide as many secrets as the hangar in the desert. It's the kind of place that manages to be both convenient and totally secret at the same time. And yes, there's a helicopter pad at the rear of the house, which currently stands empty, obviously awaiting our arrival.

"This is where we're going?" I ask. It seems impossible. Far too much to spend on a secret base. But then, the one back home wouldn't have been cheap.

Grayson nods. "This is where we're going," he agrees. "Celes, welcome to Location Two."

FIVE

The helicopter touches down, the rotors slowing to an eventual halt while I stare at them. Their whirling is almost like a meditation, giving me something to distract my thoughts from what has happened to Jack just for a moment. They come to a halt, and the pilot moves round to open the door, letting us out onto the helipad in the middle of the grand estate we saw from above.

I get out and breathe in. The air has a different feel to it here. It's not dry, like in the desert, and it doesn't have the perpetual fumes that you find with a big city like New York. Instead, the air in this place is clean, and clear, with the scents of flowering plants carried on the breeze. The light's different too. It's gentler somehow, not harsh and glaring like it was back at the Underground's base. Behind us, the manor stands imposingly, looking far larger from ground level, its façade perfectly preserved despite the ivy growing up one side of it. My main impression is of glass, thanks to the rows of windows on every level. Even the ground floor has French windows arranged in a line to let more light in.

It's from one of those sets that an older man walks, leaning on a cane. As he gets closer, I see that he is probably Sebastian Cook's age, but he looks older from a distance, thanks to the combination of the stick and his shock of white hair, which sticks up at odd angles as though he has forgotten to comb it for a few days. Even so, his posture is ramrod straight, and he's wearing tweed, which makes him look a little like the lord of the manor, out for a stroll.

When he gets closer, he stares at me, looking me up and down with obvious recognition. But then, he would have been told I was coming. "So it is true. Sebastian has succeeded in locating you. I hadn't thought he would be able to."

His voice sounds almost like an exaggeration. Jack's British accent is faint and delicious, but this man's sounds like simply too much. It's like the kind of accent you might hear from one of the characters in an old war movie, or something.

"You do not know how many years we have waited for this," He says, looking around as though he expects more than just the two of us. "Where is Dr. Cook?"

It isn't Sebastian I'm thinking of right then, but that's a reminder that there are more people than just Jack in danger. "He's still back at the Underground," I say, not trusting myself to put it more directly than that. "He... couldn't make it with us."

"And Jack? I would have expected him to be here on such an important occasion."

It's all I can do to keep from crying at that moment. I manage to shake my head. Grayson seems to sense the downturn in my mood, and puts a hand on my arm.

The white-haired man seems to pick up on it too, and I get the sense that this is someone who won't miss anything. "I shouldn't worry about Jack too much, young lady. I trained him very well, and he was a good student. He always had the drive for work as a Fader, not to mention a knack for guessing what was going to happen. He should be well equipped to deal with any situation that crops up."

"I'm sorry," I say, not wanting to lose control like this in front of a stranger.

"It's quite all right," the man replies, and then sticks out a hand. "Now we should probably be properly introduced. I am... well, my full name is Dr. Major Sir Lionel Lancaster, and then there are enough letters to play scrabble with after that," he smiled. "Please call me Lionel."

"Celes," I say, taking his hand. "Dr. Major Sir?"

"I am glad to say I have led an eventful life."

"He worked as a British military liaison with the memory fading project," Grayson supplies, "and then he helped to apply principles from it to create accelerated training methods for the Royal Marine Commandos, Parachute Regiment, Special Air Service, and Special Boat Service. Now he trains top Faders."

I look over at Grayson. He comes out with the information as though it's nothing. Something he has known all his life, yet there's no way he should have known it.

Lionel smiles, taking Grayson's hand. "That would make you Grayson, I assume. I received a message from Sebastian about you. His people obviously did a good job with your memories. But then, Sebastian always was a genius. It made those of us who got to observe the project simply because we happened to have a background in the sciences, feel quite jealous. And of course, he has always been a man with his heart in the right place. Unlike some."

I wince. "The Others got him," I say. "I'm not sure if he will be-"

"Oh, Sebastian will be fine for now," Lionel says dismissively. "In fact, I wouldn't be surprised if his capture were one of the major objects of their raid."

"So they weren't going after me?" I ask.

"I am sure they were," Lionel says, "but a good planner will always try to achieve a lot with a little. You are valuable, of course, but Sebastian? His wealth of knowledge is priceless. He knows the details of constructing the memory fading machine, for example, along with so many other secrets that the Others will simply *have* to keep him alive."

I feel the faintest ray of hope then. Not just for Sebastian, but for Jack as well. "So the Others...won't kill him?"

"Not if he is of use to them. And he will be. The Underground is no longer extant in that location, and they do not know where the machine went. Sebastian will be needed to either locate it or rebuild it."

I have to ask. "What about Jack? What if they capture him?"

Lionel looks grave for a moment. "That is a much more difficult situation, young lady, though hopefully, Jack would not allow it to come to that."

I can't bring myself to say that Jack appeared to be on the verge of capture when we left. Not now. "What would happen?"

"If the Others know what he is..." he looks over at me, and it's clear that the middle-aged Englishman knows exactly what I am "...then I'm afraid they would probably kill him out of hand."

"And if they don't?" I ask, trying to cling onto any scrap of hope.

"Then Jack is still a potential threat, who has killed many of their people over the years. I'm sorry to say that they might well still execute him."

I let out a breath, and feel Grayson's arm slip around me protectively. I know what he feels about Jack. I know he won't care about that news, but he's there for me. He's there to make sure that I can still stand, even though it doesn't feel like there's anything left in the world for me.

"Let's get you inside," Lionel says. "You're here, and you should have the chance to get your bearings before anything else happens."

He leads the way, and I follow, not knowing what else to do. The inside of the manor house is odd. There are rooms there that don't feel like they've been touched for a hundred years, while others have a very modern look to them, with plenty of glass and brushed steel mixed in with the rest of the furniture. It reminds me a lot of the apartment Jack had to blow up shortly after meeting me.

"This is an interesting place you have here," I manage to say.

"Oh, I do my best with it," Lionel returns. "I have to keep some of the older stuff for the look of an old English manor house, but it isn't really to my taste."

No, it's Jack's, and it's hard to understand until I remember the comment about Lionel training him. Jack has obviously picked up a lot from the man who was once his mentor, even down to his taste in decorating.

Grayson and I follow Lionel as he shows us around the various rooms on the ground floor. They are fairly typical of what I would have expected from a manor house like this. There's a library, a large kitchen, a gallery. It's only when Lionel leads us down a flight of stairs that I start to realize there's more to the place.

"This used to be a wine cellar, until we made a few alterations and... well, extended things a bit."

That's an understatement. The stairs lead down to a corridor almost identical to those back at the Underground's main base. There are doors leading off it, and Lionel pushes them open as we pass. In the first, there are people working, huddled over screens as they tap away at keyboards. The second door features what appears to be a shooting range, where a couple of people are practicing with pistols. A third features a large, matted area, where a couple of Faders are going back and forth, exchanging blows and trying to throw one another. Lionel pauses there, going over to correct one of the combatants, and tripping him casually when he isn't expecting it.

"There. Maybe now you'll remember that this isn't a game, young man." He comes back and apologizes. "Sorry about that. People these days never seem to understand that there aren't any rules in a real fight until you demonstrate it to them first hand."

Lionel seems satisfied enough to move on then, taking us into an elevator, which leads us down to a lower floor. There, he spends several seconds getting us through voice print and retinal scan based locks, which let us into what appears to be a control room, where we are surrounded by screens. Those screens show all kinds of things, from news feeds to satellite imagery of distant locations. There are pictures of people, along with information about them, as well as graphs that make no sense without being told what they are about. There is even some footage that looks like it is being taken directly from security cameras and overhead drones.

One of the screens shows the hangar I had thought of as the Underground's only base until recently. It's in ruins, the fires having burned themselves out. It's eerily quiet, and there's no sign of anyone still being there. There aren't even any bodies on the ground from where the battle occurred. It's just deserted.

"What happened to everyone?" I ask. "Did the Others kill them all?"

Lionel shakes his head. "We were able to evacuate the majority of the personnel from Location Six, along with the files and equipment that were most sensitive. It looks like Sebastian was also able to activate the self-destruction sequence, eliminating anything that could have been used by the Others."

"But that doesn't make sense," I say. "How could they have evacuated before the explosion? I was there. There were a few Faders fighting the Others, and Sebastian was there, but I didn't see anyone else come out of the place."

"That's because they left via a different route," Lionel explains. "There is more than one reason they call us the Underground, you know."

SIX

"So you're saying they escaped underground somehow?" I say.

Lionel nods. He's still looking at the screen that shows the broken and ruined Underground base. He taps a few keys on a nearby computer keyboard, apparently making a note of something.

"As you probably know, each of our bases has multiple underground levels. We are, for example, currently some four stories underground."

"We are?" I ask. I don't know why, but somehow, it's easier to imagine a maze of tunnels beneath a hangar like the one back in the desert than it is to imagine them beneath an old house like this. And it's not like I can tell just by looking how far down we are. There aren't any windows here, but beyond that, this control center could be on any level.

"The Underground got the idea from the kind of underground tunnels and bunkers used in this country during the Second World War," Lionel explains. "There were whole secret sections that did their work underground then, and sections of the London tube system were used as part of it. There were also plenty of bunkers and tunnels built for use in the event of an invasion. This house originally had several like that, which we merely expanded and made a little more appropriate for our needs."

"Just how big are these tunnels?" I ask, trying to get some sense of the scale on which the Underground is working.

Lionel shrugs. "They are extensive enough to hide our whole operation in each location. We really don't want to draw attention to ourselves. Not only does that create an increased risk of attack by the Others, but even local governments tend to get quite worried when they see heavily armed operations on our scale. It wouldn't do to give them an excuse to send in troops, now would it?"

I guess not, though I hadn't really thought about it like that. "Don't you work with governments?" I ask.

"Our relationships with them can be quite... complicated," Lionel says. "Most of those like myself and Sebastian came out of official programs of one kind or another, yet no government would ever admit to doing the kinds of things we look into. If we were officially linked to any one government, that might cause embarrassment, as well as creating the illusion that we are here to support one country's interests, rather than simply to do research. On the whole, it is better for us to be merely a private organization with a few friends in high places, don't you think?"

I can't answer that. In fact, all it does is to remind me just how out of my depth I am. I'm a part of this world because of what I am, but I am not trained for it, and I don't have any experience of trying to keep up with its complex politics. Instead, I try to latch onto something simpler.

"So these tunnels beneath the various bases include escape tunnels?" I ask.

"They do," Lionel says, then turns to Grayson. "Tell me, young man, where does the tunnel from Location Six come out?"

"In the mountains," Grayson says, and then gives Lionel a map reference.

For a moment, the retired major looks thoughtful. "Sebastian certainly put a lot more information into you than I would have thought," he says. "It's enough to make me wonder why. Still, you're correct."

He taps another few computer keys, and one of the cameras switches its view until it shows what appears to be nothing more than a mountainside.

"I don't see what we're looking at," I say.

"Be patient," Lionel advises. "Ah, there. Thank goodness."

The camera zooms in, and because I know that there must be something there, I try to see what Lionel is seeing. It's only when the hatch in the rock face starts to swing open though that I even notice it. It opens wide like some kind of modern day take on Aladdin's cave, and from that gap in the rock, people start to appear.

They come out in ones and twos, looking organized and determined. Most are holding bags, or carrying rucksacks. The only ones who aren't are the ones who appear to be injured. I recognize Marlene among their number, and I feel a little surge of gladness that at least some of those who have helped me have survived.

"What's in the bags?" Grayson asks.

Lionel shrugs. "Information, weaponry, personal effects. Whatever they could grab, I should imagine. There is a lot of material kept at each base, and in the event of destruction, it would need to be transferred securely."

"Couldn't you just do that online?" I ask, and find myself feeling stupid when Lionel looks at me. "What?"

"That kind of transfer could easily be intercepted," he says. "If one of the bases is under attack physically, then we have to assume that it would be attacked by hackers simultaneously, all ready to intercept any packets of information sent out from the site. No, it is far safer to move things physically. My only worry in that regard is whether the Others might be able to retrieve anything from the systems damaged by the destruction sequence."

"Mr. Cook incorporated a controlled EMP effect into the sequence specifically to prevent that," Grayson says. I still can't get used to the idea that he knows this stuff. "It would have been contained within the base by the outer shielding, but would have wiped all electronic storage."

"Well, that's something, I suppose," Lionel says, returning his attention to the screen. More people are spilling from the hole in the rock. Most of them are on foot, but a few ride motorcycles, skirting around the edge of the group with weapons at the ready. I guess that they're those Faders who remained behind to supervise the evacuation rather than going out to face the Others with Jack.

The three of us watch that screen, looking, waiting, hoping. It's obvious to me that we're all looking for the same thing, but none of us says it. We're all hoping that Sebastian or Jack's face will miraculously show up among those coming out of the base. That things will somehow be all right in spite of what I saw from the helicopter as we were leaving.

As time goes on though, and more faces go past without any sign of them, my hopes diminish. And when the door in the rock slams shut without them having appeared, those hopes wither and die. If they aren't in that group, it's because they couldn't be. Which means that they didn't get away when they fought the Others.

"So that's it," I say. "They're... gone."

"We don't know that for certain," Grayson says. I know he's trying to be comforting, and I appreciate the effort, but I can't help remembering that it was he who shoved me into the helicopter, he who sedated me with a syringe full of who knows what.

"What do you care?" I demand. "It's not like you even like Jack."

"I care that it hurts you," Grayson says, trying to put his arm around me again.

I shrug him off. "But you wouldn't be upset if he were dead, would you?"

"That isn't fair, Celes."

I shake my head. "No, what isn't fair is that Jack is probably dead. That or captured, and from the sounds of it, the Others wouldn't keep him alive for long. What isn't fair is that there were only two seats on the helicopter, and suddenly you knew so much that they couldn't risk leaving you behind."

"So you'd rather they captured me?" Grayson demands.

"Your father wouldn't have hurt you, Grayson. He'll kill Jack though."

"That was before," Grayson says. "Now... now I have a bunch of stuff in my head I didn't have before. I know things I shouldn't know. I can do things I shouldn't be able to do. Now, I don't even know who I am, so how is my father really going to react to me. I wish this situation didn't have to be like this, Celes, but it is-"

"And Jack and Sebastian are either dead or captured," I finish for him.

Lionel pats me on the shoulder then. It's a slightly stiff, awkward seeming gesture for him, but he does it. "Now, we don't know that for certain, young lady. Jack remains a very resourceful agent, while Sebastian is a highly intelligent man. It may be that they were able to come up with a solution to their situation that we simply haven't been able to think of."

"But it isn't very likely," I say.

Lionel shakes his head. "You mustn't give up hope like that. As I said, Jack is a highly skilled Fader, and he has gotten out of tight spots in the past."

I want to believe him. I do. I can still remember the ease with which Jack got us away from his apartment when the Others showed up there. The way he tracked me down to save me and Grayson when we were being chased along the highway. It's just that the circumstances seem so hopeless that I can't see how even Jack could possibly get out of them.

I open my mouth to say something, and an alarm goes off. Lionel's head whips round, and he taps something into his keyboard. Instantly, the screens around us change, becoming an outline map of Europe with a dark background. Mostly dark, anyway. There are spots of brightness here and there, mostly not very intense. There's a brighter one in the south of England, and another brighter one further away, on the continent.

"What is this?" I ask.

"This is the display for our main scanners," Lionel explains. "The ones that allowed us to identify you, and which have allowed us to explore a number of other… phenomena over the years. You see the bright spots? Each one represents something that the Underground would need to investigate further."

"Why are some of the spots brighter than others?" I ask.

"That is simply a question of signal strength."

I remember then what Sebastian told me back at the Underground's other base. "And I give off a strong signal, right?"

"Exactly." Lionel jabs his finger at the first of the bright dots. The one in England. "This one is you, Celes. Or at least the signal our scanners pick up of you. This one…" he moves his finger to the other glowing spot "…this one is new. And it's intense, if it's enough to set off the alarm."

"So that's emitting the same kind of signal Celes did?" Grayson asks.

"That would appear to be the case, yes," Lionel says. He sounds like he wants to be excited, but is restraining himself from letting too much of it show with a certain amount of difficulty. "It also appears to be of a similar strength. Which suggests that there may be something else like you out there."

He says it so calmly that the implications don't sink in for a moment or two. "There's someone else like me out there?" I ask.

Lionel nods. "That's what it looks like, at least."

"Where?"

I need to know. I need to know that I am not alone. That there might actually be some answers for me out there somewhere. Lionel looks at the map, then taps in yet more instructions to the computer. A more detailed map overlays itself on the first one.

"It looks like Switzerland to me."

SEVEN

Lionel stares at the computer screen for a moment or two longer, then pulls out a phone and started speaking into it.

"How soon can you have a full team ready to fly? We have a signal. Twenty minutes? Good. Switzerland. Yes, I know. We'll be taking them with us."

By 'them' I guess that he means me and Grayson. That guess is confirmed almost as soon as Lionel puts his phone away.

"Come on," he says. "Looks like you are not going to get much of a rest here. We can't very well leave you behind while we're all off chasing after things in Switzerland, so you're going to have to come with us. The helicopters will be touching down shortly."

Lionel doesn't give us a chance to say anything, but leads the way up, back out of the base. There are Faders waiting for us as we reach the surface, all armed, and all dressed in cold weather gear. One, a woman in her mid-twenties, tosses warm coats to both Grayson and me.

"If we're heading into the alps," she says, in an accent not as pronounced as Lionel's, but somewhere closer to Jack's, "then it could get cold quickly, just with the altitude. You'll want to wrap up."

Helicopters arrive. There are two of them; big dual rotor things that look like they're built for long distance travel. Grayson, Lionel, a couple of Faders and I get on the first of them, while the remainder take the second. It hardly seems like we've been in England any time at all, and already we're leaving.

The journey is a long one, and despite the design of the helicopters, we have to stop several times to refuel. At each stop, Lionel gets out to talk to local officials, and they quickly hurry to help. It seems that the middle-aged man has quite a lot of connections.

One thing the journey does is give me time to think. I'm not sure if that's a good thing, because it's too easy for my thoughts to slide back to Jack, and what has happened to him, yet I manage to distract myself for at least some of the journey with thoughts of what might be waiting for us. Lionel has already said that the signal is similar to the one the Underground's sensors get from me, so does that mean that there's someone else like me out there somewhere, living their life in some pretty little Swiss village? That thought seems like too much to hope for, but I can't help thinking about what it would be like to meet someone else with my strange talents. Someone else who *knows* what it's like to be me.

The Swiss Alps are beautiful. They're also, as the Fader who gave us the coats predicts, cold. I guess that's why some places there can offer year round skiing. That's not what we're there for though, and we fly with purpose, following Lionel's instructions as he stares at the screen of a laptop. We fly around for what feels like forever before he points a finger at a mountain slope.

"There. Take us down there. The signal is coming from that direction."

The pilot takes the helicopter down, managing to find enough flat land to touch down on. The other helicopter lands beside us. From ground level, it's easy to see the cave that cuts into the mountainside, though it was impossible to spot from above.

"Check it out," Lionel says to the woman Fader, and she nods. In seconds, all the Faders are off the helicopters, all with pistols or heavier weapons drawn. It seems they aren't taking any chances.

"Shouldn't we go with them?" I suggest.

Lionel shakes his head. "We wait here and monitor things until we know it is safe."

"What could possibly go wrong?" I ask.

I get an answer to that almost immediately. The sound of gunfire comes from the cave, along with shouts and barked orders. Grayson has a gun in his hand, I don't know where it has come from, while his other arm is on mine, preventing me from running towards the sound. He knows me well enough to know that I need to know what is going on.

I find out quickly enough. The woman whom Lionel had ordered into the cave runs out from it, wounded in the side. She's been shot. She makes it over to the helicopter.

"What happened, Annette?" Lionel asks.

The woman's face is ashen. "It was a fake signal. The Others... they're in there."

I start to leap down from the helicopter, but Lionel grabs me and pulls me back with surprising strength for a man his age.

"Grayson?" he says, making a question of it. Grayson seems to understand, even though I don't, and hops down from the helicopter. Why is he allowed to do it when I'm not?

"You and Annette need to hold the perimeter around the cave mouth. Kill any of the Others who make an appearance."

They move back towards the cave mouth, and Grayson shoots at something inside. Lionel looks to the cockpit of the helicopter.

"Pilot? Prepare for takeoff."

"Takeoff?" the word is out of my mouth almost instantly. "You're planning to just leave Grayson and the others behind?"

"I'm planning to get you to safety, you stupid girl. We've been set up. Besides, there's another helicopter."

"I don't care, about that," I say. "Get Grayson in here now, because I'm not leaving him!"

Before he can do anything to stop me, I'm out of the helicopter. The biting cold of the Alpine mountainside cuts into me, but I don't care. I've already lost Jack. I'm not about to lose Grayson too. He and Annette are by the entrance, exchanging fire with people inside the cave I assume to be the Others. For the briefest of instants, I think that they might actually be containing them, but it's clear that they aren't when a hail of gunfire comes back at us, and we're forced to hit the floor.

"There are too many," Annette says, and I have to admire her stoicism. She hasn't said anything about the bullet wound in her side. "Get ready to retreat back to the helicopter. On three. One. Two. Three!"

She fires a quick series of shots into the cave, then grabs my arm as she runs for the helicopter. Except that the one we came in is in the air, hovering neatly, with Lionel Lancaster in the open doorway, a vicious looking machine gun in his hands.

It roars over our heads, and several of the Others who leave the cave in that moment are cut down. Meanwhile, I find myself half dragged to the second helicopter, where the pilot is already powering up the engines.

"Get us out of here," Annette says to the pilot. It sounds like exactly what we should be doing in that moment.

Except that somehow, I know we can't leave. There's something... almost pulling me back towards the cave.

"Wait!"

Annette looks at me. "This is no time to wait. I'm wounded, and there's only so long the major will be able to lay down suppressing fire. The whole operation is a waste of time, and we need to go."

"That's just it," I say. "There's something there. I'm sure of it. I can *feel* it."

"You can feel it?" Annette says. "I'm not risking your life on a feeling. This is a trick by the Others, and nothing more. The major would have my hide if I let anything happen to you."

"No," I say, moving to the edge of the helicopter. "Please wait. I have to see this. I'll jump if I have to."

Annette's face creases in pain. "And then I'd have to jump off and drag you back. You are *not* making my day any easier, you know."

"I know," I say, feeling slightly ashamed. This woman has gotten herself shot over this, after all. "And I'm sorry, but I'm right about this, I know I am."

"Oh, for... pilot, get the major on coms. Now please."

"Lionel here," the voice comes out of speakers. "What's going on down there, Annette?"

"Celes here thinks that there's something real in the cave, sir. She's refusing to leave. I need further instructions."

"Well then, take off."

Grayson chooses that moment to speak up. "Dr. Lancaster, I've known Celes for most of her life. When she's stubborn like this, she usually has a good reason."

"You're sure?"

"Yes, sir."

Lionel makes an irritated sound over the speakers. "Oh, very well, I think I got most of the blighters with the Browning anyway."

Annette nods. "Understood, major. I'll cover her as she goes in. Over and out." She passes me a pistol. "Jack tells me you're good with one of these."

She knows Jack? No, I don't have time to think about that.

"I can use it," I say.

"Good, then stay close to me, do as you're told, and maybe we won't all be killed. I just hope you're right, that's all."

Annette, Grayson and I hop out of the helicopter, moving towards the cave. The Fader moves slowly, haltingly, and I wonder how much blood she has lost. She's wary, her gun extended before her ready for the slightest hint of a threat. Yet we don't come up against any opposition. There are bodies though, laying on the floor wherever they have fallen. Some are Faders, while some are obviously the Others.

I'm not looking at them. Instead, as my eyes adjust to the semi-dark of the cave, I find myself wondering why it *is* only semi-dark. It's then that I realize it. There's something glowing towards the back of the cave. I move towards it quickly. Almost as soon as I do though, it stops.

"I have a torch here somewhere," Annette announces. That makes me smile, because even though I know she's just using the English word for a flashlight, it makes me think of explorers wandering through caves with flaming torches.

Her flashlight illuminates the cave a little, and we move back, trying to get a better view. Almost as soon as we do, the glow returns, and now I can see what it's coming from. It's emanating from a rock, which is almost spherical, and looks a bright gold in the darkness of the rest of the cave.

Annette reaches out for it, putting away her gun.

"I really wouldn't touch it, if I were you, Annette."

I know that voice. I've been daydreaming about that voice for most of the last day. I've been wondering if I'll ever hear it again, and trying to work out what I'll say if I do. I almost don't dare to turn around, but I do. In front of me is a tall figure, his face hooded and hidden by a scarf, wrapped up against the cold.

"Jack!"

"Celes," Gray's hand stops me before I can run to him. "You don't know for certain if it's…"

But I know, and a second later, I have the proof. Jack removes his hood, and pulls down the scarf, letting me see the features I've wanted to see since I left the desert. Even by the light of a single flashlight and a glowing rock, it can't be anyone else.

"Celes." He almost whispers it.

"Jack."

EIGHT

Grayson can't hold me back then. I run to Jack. I have to see him. I have to hold him. I know it will disappoint Grayson, even if they have taken the memories of us together from him, but I can't hold back. Not when I've spent so much of the last day or so wondering if Jack was alive or dead.

I fall into his arms, wanting to kiss him so badly, so urgently that I can barely stop myself. I only manage it because I'm all too aware of Grayson standing there, and there are some things I don't want to do in front of him. So I hold him by the dim light of the cave, looking up into those clear blue eyes of his.

Jack doesn't seem as willing to hold back as I am. He bends down to kiss me, and when he does, I don't stop him. I need this. I need to feel it. To know that it's real. His lips meet mine, and for several long seconds I'm caught up in the moment, caught up in just kissing Jack back until I can't do anything else.

When we pull apart, I'm actually out of breath from it. "Jack…I thought…I thought you were…"

"Dead," Jack says. "I know. I'm sorry. For a moment or two there, *I* thought I was."

"So how did you escape?" I ask. It hardly seems possible that Jack could have gotten away from the situation we left him in.

Jack shakes his head. "It's a long story. One I promise I'll tell you someday, but right now…"

"Now we have to get out of here!" Lionel's voice booms from behind us all. He's still carrying his machine gun, slung over his back in a way that doesn't really fit with the rest of him. He has to have run from the helicopter to have gotten here this quickly. "Or had you forgotten the Others? They will be sending more people out here when they can't get anyone to answer their communications." He glances over to Jack, giving the other man a brief nod of acknowledgement. "Good to see you back, boy. I knew you had it in you."

"Thank you, sir."

Lionel shakes his head. "This is a tough business all round."

I look at the bodies lying in the cave, Faders and Others both. Tough doesn't begin to cover it. The last few days have been brutal, deadly. Senseless. Why do the Others need to hunt me like this? Why do they feel they have to risk so many lives? What is it about me that threatens them so much they would rather see carnage like this than just let me live my life?

"Anyway," Lionel says, "we need to go."

Annette, who is currently trying to put pressure on the wound in her side, looks from Lionel to the glowing rock. "What are we going to do about that?" she asks. "Are we taking it with us, or leaving it, or what?"

Jack steps close to it, kneeling beside it. "We need to be careful," he says. "This is a source of intense energy."

He points to one of the closest bodies to the rock. It could be one of the Others, or it could be one of the Faders. It's hard to tell. Unlike the bodies cut down by bullets, this one is charred and blackened, burned almost beyond recognition. I know what Jack's implying. This body looks just like the ones of the Others I have killed with the energy inside me. It's the same. Powerfully, dangerously the same.

Whatever this rock is, it has to do with what I am. With what both Jack and I are.

Lionel understands too, because he moves to stare at the rock. "This has a connection to Celes here, I take it?"

I can only nod. "It's the same effect I get when..." I can't finish that.

"Yes," Lionel says. "I have seen the reports. Not to mention the footage in the archives. So, this is where the signal came from. I imagine you must be disappointed."

"Disappointed?"

"That it isn't from a person." Lionel looks at the rock a little more closely, though he's careful not to touch it.

I hadn't thought about that, but I nod. "A little. But this is still... it's still something."

"It is indeed. We will need to study it further. Though we will have to be careful." He looks at the burned up figure. "I imagine, since they were here first, that this was one of the Others. It would have been the first person to touch the rock. After that, they would have stayed around, trying to work out how to deal with it, and that would have been when we arrived."

"So they were here before we came, following the same signal," Grayson says. "It wasn't a set up. No one knew the Underground would show up."

"Exactly," Jack replies. "And since they didn't expect anyone, they'll think it's just the rock when the bodies turn out to be completely burned up or buried in an avalanche."

Lancaster smiles and puts an arm around Jack. "Always one step ahead, Jack. Still the same Jack, but better. I have enough explosives in the helicopter."

Jack looks over at me, and I can see the love there. It's intense, a heat almost as great as the one coming from the rock, and I can feel heat rising in me in answer to it. Literal heat, of the kind I've used to kill people. I look away quickly. It's true then, what Grayson implied back when he was asking why I only burned people up around Jack. Jack's my trigger. My feelings for him help to spark this power. And they have grown so much.

"I'm better now because I have a reason to be," Jack says. He moves over to me. Right now, I'm not sure that's such a good idea, but it seems he isn't planning to kiss me again right away. I don't know whether to be disappointed or not by that.

"Celes," Jack says. "We know that your power doesn't cause you any harm. You're connected to this rock, so you should be able to handle it safely. I think you're the only one who can."

"What if you're wrong?" Grayson asks, but he's too late.

I've already bent to pick up the rock. It's warm, but it's a pleasant warmth, like holding another body to me as I lift it into my arms. It's big enough that I have to cradle it two handed.

"Do you have any idea how dangerous that was?" Grayson demands.

I shake my head. "It's fine, Grayson. *I'm* fine."

And then it happens. The rock flares. It flares so bright that for a moment I think it is incinerating me. I think that my last moment will have been spent arguing with Grayson, and that in less than a second, I'll be another charred corpse on the floor of the cave. I feel the energy pouring into me; more and more, until it feels like I'll burst with it.

Then, just as quickly as the rock flared up, it stops.

"Did you see that?" Annette asks.

"You just absorbed it," Jack says. He sounds almost as shocked as the female Fader.

Lionel looks at me closely, then at the rock. "Hmm... it appears to have been rendered inert. I think you are correct, Jack. I think Celes here has absorbed the energy of the rock, though I for one won't be touching it until we have run a lot more tests. Would you mind carrying it back to the helicopter, Celes?"

I do it, depositing the rock in a box in the back where no one can touch it accidentally. It's close enough that I can watch it, imagine it in there. Jack comes to sit alongside me as we take off, his hand over mine.

"Can you imagine it, Jack?" I ask, unable to keep the excitement out of my voice. "This rock is part of where we came from. It has to be. It's a link to that."

"It's...Lionel will study it. My father will, too, once we get him away from the others. This is potentially a very important find."

"Assuming that there's anything left of it," I say, as the helicopter pulls its way up into the air.

"Even then. Then we'll find out more about you, me, and the planet we're meant to be from. Don't worry, Celes."

Jack kisses my temple, tracing his fingers along my chin and tilting it up so that I'm looking deep into his eyes. "I thought I'd never see you again, Celes, and that thought alone was the scariest thought I've ever had. The thought of getting killed was nothing compared to that." Jack closes his eyes and looks down. It's the rawest I've seen of emotions on his face. "I don't ever want to experience that again, Celes. I love you too much to risk that again. Even when I got here, near to the rock, all I could think of then was you. You're everything to me."

I know how he feels, because I feel the same way. Yet right then, in the helicopter, I can't tell him. Grayson is only a few feet away. Or he was. I see that he has gone to the other side of the helicopter, where he's helping Annette to keep pressure on her wound. The bleeding seems to have stopped. She's been lucky. And Grayson... Grayson is obviously avoiding me.

Have I hurt him that much with this, or is he just being considerate? Is he just making it easy for me to be here with Jack by leaving us as alone as he can in such a confined space? I don't know. He's always been so understanding, yet that very understanding is enough to make me feel a little guilty about Jack. When Jack touches my face again, I know I can't just kiss him. Not here. Not like this. Back In the cave was enough. Instead, I try to find a way to distract Jack.

"How is Sebastian?" I ask him. "He didn't get away?"

Jack looks like I've just slapped him. Maybe he wasn't expecting me to shoot down his attempts to get close to me so thoroughly, or maybe it's the mention of his father. Whichever one it is, it's enough to make his expression slide back to that coolly professional one he has down so well.

"The Others have him, but he was well when I left. Richard, his old colleague, wants him to work for them."

"But he won't do that, will he?" I ask.

Jack shakes his head. "Not willingly. Which means that they'll either have to find ways to put pressure on him to do it, or they'll have to give up."

Putting pressure on him doesn't sound pleasant. "And if they give up, what happens then?" I ask. "They don't just let him go, presumably."

Jack shakes his head. "They'd kill him. But we have time. They won't do that until they've exhausted every way of getting to the information about the memory extractors."

"We can't let him stay there, though."

"No," Jack says, "which is why we're going to break him free as soon as we get back."

NINE

It takes us a while to fly back to Location Two. With the rock successfully recovered, there isn't the rush that there was getting there. We're able to take things slowly, even stopping long enough for Annette to get medical attention. We make it back as night is falling, landing quietly outside the old house and going in to meet the Faders there.

Their mood is somber, but then, they have just lost almost ten of their colleagues in one mission. What would it be like if I lost ten of my friends in one day? If they were walking around, laughing and joking one moment and then dead the next. And this is all because of what I am. They must hate me.

Jack seems to get what I'm feeling, because he puts an arm around me.

"It's what they signed on for, Celes," he says. "Everyone who becomes a Fader knows the risks, and accepts them."

"Even you, Jack?" I ask. "Would you have been a Fader if it weren't for your father, I mean?"

Jack nods. "I would. This isn't just about my father for me. There's who I am. *What* I am. There's what happened to my mother, too. And what we do here is important. I'm convinced of that. Especially after being assigned to protect you. If the Underground didn't exist, the Others would be free to kill you, and that... I don't want to think about that."

Jack takes me to a bedroom in the base, where he says I can rest, and leaves, though he seems reluctant to do so. "I have to go and talk to the others about the rescue mission," he says. "Try to get some rest."

I do, drifting into fitful sleep. I'm woken a little while later by a hand shaking my shoulder. It's Annette, the Fader who came with us to Switzerland. She's wearing a top that leaves her midriff bare, under an open dark shirt. That exposes a set of bandages on her side to the open air.

"Does that hurt?" I ask, sitting up.

"Only a little. Jack sent me to fetch you. We're meeting to discuss the rescue, and Lionel wants you in on it. Well... no, he wants *Jack* in on it, and Jack won't leave you alone, so it looks like you're coming. Come on."

Annette leads the way, not down, but up into the main house, into an elegant drawing room where Lionel, Grayson and Jack are already sitting on ancient looking armchairs, talking.

"This is potentially very dangerous, Jack," Lionel points out.

"I know that, sir, but you agree that it needs to happen?"

The ex-military man nods. "Sebastian is too valuable to leave in the Others' hands." He looks up at me. "Hello Celes, Annette. Please sit down, both of you."

We take seats, and Lionel continues. "The necessity of the mission does not make it less dangerous, however. We lost a lot of good people today. Too many to mount an immediate full scale mission without additional support."

"That's why I think we should use some of the Faders who had to flee Location Six. They will be able to boost our numbers, and they'll be close enough to help with the operation."

"So the Others' headquarters are in the US?" I ask.

Jack nods. "Though it's not an easy location to assault. It's not well away from everywhere, like Location Six was. They prefer to put their bases in ordinary houses, in suburbs and near schools, malls, homes."

"It makes it easy to fit in," Annette says.

"It also means that civilians could be hurt in any full scale assault," Jack shoots back. "So we need to be careful."

"Where exactly are they located?" Lionel asks.

"Virginia," Jack replies. "Near Celes' house, in fact." Jack pauses then, as though wondering whether to say what he's thinking. "It's also not too far from the location where we placed Celes' family."

My family. Will this put them in danger? Could I maybe see them? I know I can't think about that, but I don't know how to stop it. Lionel cuts into my train of thought, though.

"Then we'll also be able to get a small amount of support from Location Four. I'll contact Jonas there to let him know."

"Location Four?" I guess the name of Location Six should have given me a clue that there are a lot of Underground bases out there, but I'm having enough trouble adjusting to the scale of places like this without imagining still more of them.

"It's one of the Underground's smaller operations," Jack says. "It's mostly research and surveillance, unlike Location Six."

"Or this base," Grayson says. "Location Two is large because it's a training ground."

I look over at him. The more things like that Grayson says, the easier it is to see him as what he is now. Somehow, Sebastian has used his memory machine to make a real Fader of him.

"Talking of which," Grayson says, "I should probably get some training in. I... my mind knows what I need to do, but I'm still not sure about the rest of me."

"I'll arrange something," Annette says. "Though I hope this won't mean you'll leave me out of the mission, Major. I'm ready to go."

"You've just been shot," I point out.

"And?"

Jack speaks up then. "I think Celes is right, Annette. You should probably stay here for this one."

Annette looks over to Lionel pleadingly, but the older man shakes his head. "Jack is right. You're out for this one. In fact, there won't be many people here we can take. A few of the advanced trainers, perhaps, but mostly Location Two is full of trainees who aren't mission ready. Perhaps if I'd thought of that, the casualty count on the last operation wouldn't have been so high."

Annette starts to argue, but Lionel cuts her off. "This is my decision to make, Annette."

The Fader hangs her head, obviously upset about it, but apparently unwilling to argue further. "Yes, Major."

Lionel looks over at Jack. "Give me the location, and I'll start to arrange things. I'll let you know what we have available to us, and we can work out a more detailed tactical scenario from there. Annette, why don't you arrange that training for Grayson now?"

Annette nods, and I hear her mutter something about it being all she's good for, apparently, but she leads Grayson from the room. Lionel heads off, apparently to make a few important phone calls, which leaves me in the room with Jack.

"Don't worry about Grayson," Jack says. "Location Two is a good place to train."

"Do all Locations serve a specific purpose?" I ask.

Jack nods. "Most of them. I like Location Two though. I spent a lot of time here. I came here at sixteen, straight from school, looking to be a Fader. The Major agreed to let me start training, but forced me to stay at school into the sixth form too, so that I had the option of going on to university. I learned a lot from him."

"He seems like an amazing man," I agree. "Was this where they Faded you?"

Jack shakes his head. "All the bases have basic surveillance and signal interception capabilities, but Fading is purely done in Location Six. It's my father's specialty."

"So that's why they attacked Location Six," I say. "They want the memory device."

Jack nods. "And that's why they'll go to any lengths to get the information about it from my father. He's strong, but everyone breaks eventually. My only hope at the moment is that they won't trust to... aggressive methods to get information on something that complex, because they wouldn't be able to trust the fine detail."

"You mean torture, don't you?"

When he nods, I can't help swallowing slightly. It's a reminder of how harsh the secret world the Underground works in is. I can see the worry on Jack's face too. I haven't seen him show this much emotion about his father before. It's enough to make me want to reassure him, so I reach out to put a hand on his shoulder.

"I'm sure everyone is trying their best to get him back safe. I mean, you *know* how much they're doing, because you're helping to plan it."

I turn the hand on Jack's shoulder into a one armed hug. It's a nice sensation, and I turn my face towards his ever so slightly. Our eyes meet.

That's when I feel it again. The burning power I have brought out only a couple of times before is rising up in me, making me feel like I'm glowing from the inside. A second later, and I'm really glowing, because I can see the painfully bright light coming out of my skin, pouring from me in golden waves. For a moment, it feels perfect, but then I realize what that feeling might mean. I remember the faces of the men I've killed, and what they looked like in the seconds after I touch them. I start to jerk back. I won't burn Jack. I can't burn Jack.

It's only as I pull away that I see that Jack is glowing too. Not as much as me, but he's glowing. His eyes are golden, the way mine are when the power comes into me, and his skin is almost luminous. He doesn't let me pull away the way I want to, pulling me back, pulling me into a kiss. It's… amazing. I can feel the energy in that kiss, pulsing between us, moving through me. It's warm, and loving, feeling like I'm immersed in gently heated water, with nothing else around me. It feels like I could float in it forever. Except that I can't. Eventually, of course, the kiss has to end. We have to move away from one another.

We pull apart, and the feeling fades. The glow in Jack disappears, and the energy in me quiets down.

Jack smiles, looking at me. "I wasn't expecting that. From the looks of it, when you and I are… emotional, the energy of what we are feeds off it, becoming stronger."

I nod, and can't help returning his smile. "You were glowing too. It seems like your mother's side is beginning to emerge in you."

"I know," Jack says. "I'm not sure what that means."

"Whatever it means," I promise, "I'll be here. Remember, I've been there."

Jack kisses me again, gently. There's no rush of energy this time, but it's still a nice kiss. "I can't get enough of you, Celes. You're the only one I've ever felt this much for, even when I try to rein in my emotions. It's probably only because of that I was able to reach this point at all. You've helped me, Celes."

"I know, and I feel everything you feel, Jack."

For a moment, Jack looks happy. About as happy as it's possible for one man to be. Then his expression changes to something more serious. "We have to be careful though, Celes. We've already let too many people see us kissing and being close, but that's fine if they think that it's not serious. There are too many people who would look at us and see what we feel as a weakness to exploit. They would use our feelings against us."

I nod. "I won't let the Others see us."

Jack leans close, lowering his voice to a whisper. "I'm not just talking about the Others. We have to be careful, even in Location Two."

TEN

It takes Lionel and the others another couple of hours to make preparations. I guess important, life or death missions aren't something you can rush. Even so, it's frustrating being stuck there, knowing that every moment we waste is another moment Sebastian has to spend as a prisoner.

If it's bad for me, it's far worse for Jack. He tries to distract himself by talking to me and spending time with me, but even so, I can see the worry in him starting to creep through. Several times, he leaves me to check on how the preparations are coming, and each time, I get the feeling that he'd send us off on the mission right then if he had his way.

Eventually though, we're ready to go. That means yet another private plane ride, and we take the helicopters to a small airfield where our jet can take off. There's a small group of us going; less than a dozen, composed almost entirely of Faders in their late thirties and beyond.

Mostly beyond. When I shoot a questioning look Lionel's way and glance over to them, he seems to get the message.

"They are our master instructors," Lionel says. "As I believe I mentioned before, many of those at Location Two are simply trainees, and so are not ready for combat."

The master instructors are certainly ready. They load enough assorted weapons onto the plane to take on a small army. I hope we won't have to. I go aboard with Jack and take my seat, keeping as close to him as I can. Since the plane is a private one, there's plenty of room, but why would I want to be anywhere else?

We get airborne, winging our way across the ocean to set up the rescue. How many trips like this have I taken in the last day or two? Still, all I have to do for now is sit there and relax, so maybe it won't be so bad.

Grayson is out towards the front of the plane, working with one of the experienced Faders on combat moves. The moves themselves are simple things, from upward palm strikes to the jaw to chopping moves attacking the throat, but the speed with which the instructor makes Grayson work makes it all far more complex. When they drop to the floor of the aircraft, working on grappling moves, it's hard to even keep up with what's going on.

Maybe I should ask them for a few tips on fighting too, yet right now, I can't bring myself to move away from Jack. Right here, we can just be alone together. I reach out a hand to cover his, the way I used to when it was just Jack Simple and Celeste Channing, the young couple so deeply in love around the New York fashion scene.

I know we should be careful. I know Jack has told me that much. I even know that I don't want to flaunt our relationship around Grayson. Yet none of that matters right now. Even Grayson doesn't matter, because half the time now, it's not like he's the same Grayson he was before. Maybe, thanks to the memory device, he isn't.

One of the female Faders steps in to take over training Grayson, and she quickly has him in knots, tripping him and moving him to awkward submission holds with ease. She laughs while she does it though, and Grayson laughs too. It's only then that I realize that they're flirting as they go along. Flirting, right in the middle of their training session. And even though she's one of the younger instructors, she's still far older than Grayson. Far *too* old for Grayson. She's not even that pretty. Not really.

I look at the way I'm thinking, and I realize that I'm jealous. Pointlessly, irrationally jealous. I shouldn't be. I'm sitting here with Jack, holding onto him, being close to him. Jack's my boyfriend now, and Grayson... well, he's just someone who used to be my boyfriend. Except that it doesn't feel quite that simple. I think the problem is the way we broke up. Or rather, the way we didn't break up. We never made a clean break of the relationship, so I can't help feeling a little connected to Grayson.

Still, I put it aside as the trip goes on. We make our way over the Atlantic, and beyond, into land where farms stretch out below us in seemingly endless spaces. Jack eventually has to go talk to Lionel about what they have planned when we land. I'm not alone for long though, because Grayson takes his place. He's sweating from the workout he's had, and I'm reminded of all those times we went out running together. It seems that Grayson is too.

"Look out there, Celes," he says. "All that open space. Do you remember running together after school, just practicing?"

I nod. "Do you?" I have to know that. How much does Grayson remember? How much did they take? From what they said back at Location Six, he was only partially

Faded before he broke out. He obviously got a lot of the knowledge, and some of his memory seems to be gone, but how much?

"I remember some of it," Grayson says. "I remember running. I remember running with you. I know that we were once in a relationship together. I just can't remember the details of it." He sighs. "I kind of miss the days when things were that simple."

He reaches out for my hand. It's not the same as it was with Jack's. This is about reassurance more than anything else. I squeeze his hand back. For a moment, just a moment, I can pretend that it's the old Grayson there.

"I know," I say. "I miss those days, too. It was so much easier, and I didn't have to know all of this... stuff."

I feel him reach over to hug me, and I let him. I remember the way Grayson used to take care of so much when we were together. He was the one I would go to with problems, and he would make it feel just like everything was fine. Of course that was back before I knew all about his father, all about the Others. I know things can't go back to that, and in any case, I wouldn't want them to. I love Jack too much for that.

Grayson pulls back, looking at me seriously. "There are so many things I don't remember," he says. "You're going to think this is stupid, but I don't even remember why we broke up. I don't even remember breaking up. I know we must have, but it's just a blank for me." He shakes his head. "No, it's more than that. I feel like there's something missing that I should know. I feel... every time I see you with Jack, I feel so sad, as though I've lost something so important to me, a large part of me."

"That didn't stop you flirting with that Fader." I realize what I've just said. "Not that it makes any difference to me."

"Who? Phillipa? She's old enough to be my mother. I was just being... well, maybe I just wanted to distract myself." He looks at me intently then. "Seriously, Celes, why did we break up? What did I do?"

"Do? What makes you think you did anything wrong?" I ask, not understanding. I'm also worried. Things would be so much easier if Grayson would leave this alone. Yet I can tell that he isn't going to.

"I must have done something wrong," Grayson says, "because I don't think you would break up with someone without a good reason, Celes."

"And you're so certain that I broke up with you, rather than the other way around?"

Grayson nods. "I know that. I would *never* break up with you, even as I am now. And that's without half my memories. So you must have broken up with me instead, and there must be a reason."

"I can't explain it," I say. "Please just accept that I'm with Jack now, Grayson."

He hesitates, and I think that he wants to say that he can't accept that, but he nods. He also gets up and moves away from me, back to the other Faders. I know I should have told him the truth, but sometimes it's kinder not to, isn't it? Circumstances have torn us apart, and it would be cruel to let Grayson think he has a chance when he doesn't. I'm with Jack. I've felt a special connection to Jack almost since I met him. I'm not about to give that up.

The trouble is, while Grayson might not have his memories, I still have mine. I can still remember all the times we spent together. I can still remember wanting to run to him when my family went missing. I can still remember thinking of him, running back to him. It's more than that though. Grayson is a link to my past. The last link. Without Grayson, there's no one to remember who I was before. Without Grayson, it's like Celestra Caine never existed.

Is that a good enough reason to cling onto him though? I should let him go, shouldn't I? I should want him to be happy. So why can't I?

Eventually, the jet lands. We transfer to helicopters, and head out into that broken up farmland I saw from the air. From this angle, Virginia is beautiful. We fly for maybe twenty minutes before touching down in the middle of a small farm, nowhere near as big as the sites used for Location Two and Location Six. It's the kind of farm that looks like it must never make any real money for the owners, because it's too small. It's a few fields, and a few small outbuildings clustered around a central farmhouse, but nothing more than that.

Grayson and I haven't spoken since the plane. Instead, I sit next to Jack, using his presence like a shield to keep the rest of the world out. My life is complicated enough without Grayson deciding that he wants to get back together with me. Or learning that we never really broke up. It's better for things to be as they are. It really is.

As the helicopters touch down, we get out. The Faders move from them in well-rehearsed fashion, unloading them at speed while simultaneously checking the area for potential problems. Jack helps me out, leading me off to one side, while Lionel is the last one off. He signals to the helicopters, and they leave us there, taking off again so that in less than a couple of minutes, the farmyard is back to looking like nothing special once again.

"This is it?" I ask, speaking to Jack. He nods. "But it doesn't look like anything."

"That's kind of the point." One of the outbuilding doors opens to reveal the speaker. It's Marlene from Location Six. Her arm is heavily bandaged. She nods to me, to Jack, to Lionel. She doesn't so much as look at Grayson. I guess she's still upset about the violent way that he broke out when they tried to Fade him.

"Hello, everyone," she says. "Welcome to Location Four. Jonas is waiting for you inside."

ELEVEN

There are Faders in the farmhouse, not to mention the outbuildings, the yard... suffice it to say there are a lot of Faders there. The Underground has obviously pulled together a lot of resources in order to make this rescue mission work, with the result that there are more Faders in one place than I've seen before. Or maybe that impression is just down to the size of the farm. After all, Location Four is a lot smaller than the other Underground bases I've been too.

Marlene looks at us. "I have orders from Jonas to show the new arrivals to rooms," she says. "He thinks you'll need some rest before you move on the Fortress."

You, not we. It seems her broken arm is going to keep her out of that one. I wonder how it's doing, given that it had to be set on the way out of a base that was about to explode. When I start to mention it, though, she ignores me. She doesn't ignore Grayson, however.

"What's he doing here?" she asks. "Hasn't he done enough damage?"

Grayson looks down. "I'm sorry about your arm, but it was the only way."

Marlene ignores the apology too, looking at Jack, "I'm still looking for an explanation, Jack. What's going on? He's already given up the location of one base."

Jack shakes his head. "It isn't like that. We don't believe that Grayson had anything to do with it, anymore. It also looks like you achieved a pretty thorough Fade on him before... well, before he escaped. He's working with us, now."

"I don't like it," Marlene says.

Lionel obviously thinks it is time to intervene, because he steps forward between them. "You don't have to like it, but given the seriousness of the situation, you do have to obey instructions if we're going to get through this in one piece. Now, I believe you said that Jonas told you to show my Faders around. That includes Grayson here, so do so, please."

Marlene stares at the major for a moment, then nods tightly. "If you say so. Come on then," she says to the assembled Faders, then looks at Grayson. "And you."

They head off together, not entirely happily. I'm a little worried about Grayson going with them, because Marlene really doesn't look happy, but then, I guess I wouldn't be if I had to spend time with someone who had hurt me like that, even if I had been trying to Fade him at the time. I guess I just have to trust that the presence of the other Faders will prevent any serious problems. When they're gone, Lionel, Jack and I are left in the farmyard. We've been there a few seconds when the door to the farmhouse opens.

"There you are." The voice is a hearty one, and comes from a man making his way across the yard to us. He's a little younger than Lionel or Sebastian, good looking enough in his way, and dressed in rough work-clothes that fit in with the farm environment a lot better than anything we're wearing. He walks stiffly and it's only as he moves closer that I realize he has a prosthetic leg.

Lionel moves forward, shaking his hand vigorously and clapping him on the back in a way that suggests the two men have known one another for years. But that seems to be the thing with the Underground. It isn't some government organization pieced together from people who have never met, it's a private one, put together from people who have worked on the same kind of things for years. Of course they will know one another.

"Hello Jonas," Lionel says. "It has been too long."

The other man, Jonas, grins. "Well, we know you only get in touch when there's some impossibly difficult mission to be done. What is it this time?"

Lionel laughs at that. "Not *impossibly* difficult, I hope. I'm going to be on this one, after all."

"Ah, well it can't be as impossible as all that, then, can it? Or it won't be when you get through, anyway." Jonas waves a hand towards the farmhouse. "Why don't you head inside, Lionel? You can keep your Faders from taking up all the room in the place. It's not like I live in a mansion."

"Not still bitter about that one, are you?" Lionel asks jokingly, before going into the farmhouse. As he does, Jonas reaches up to put an arm around Jack's shoulders. Presumably, they know each other pretty well too.

"Well, now that Lionel's taken care of for now," Jonas says. "I got your message about your dad, Jack. It's a bad situation."

Jack has been sending the head of Location Four messages?

"And?" Jack asks.

Briefly, I see Jonas' eyes flicker over to me. "And I'll look into it."

"Thanks."

Jonas shakes his head. "Don't thank me. I'm interested. Exactly as you knew I would be, no doubt. This could be the breakthrough we've been working towards for years. How could I pass that up?" Jonas hesitates. "You have brought it with you, right?"

Jack nods. "Of course I've brought it with me."

I can see the look of relief on Jonas' face. Whatever Jack has brought along with him, it's obviously important. The only thing I can think of that might be that important is the rock we found. Has Jack brought that? I would have thought they'd have it under lock and key in Location Four. Lionel certainly said something about his people analyzing it.

"Good," Jonas says. "I'll have my research team begin analyzing it. If we're lucky, it will shed some light on a lot of things." He looks Jack up and down then. "How are you feeling?"

"Aside from being beaten senseless, barely escaping the Others, and having to trek halfway around the world?" Jack asked.

Jonas looks at him in a way I can't decipher. "You know what I mean."

Jack nods. "I'm fine. Better than fine. I made a breakthrough. And it's all thanks to Celes here."

"You'll have to tell me all about this breakthrough when we get a chance," Jonas says. "Along with the rest of it. It's not every day that my nephew loses his heart, and I want all the details."

"Uncle Jonas..."

"Uncle?" I ask, looking back and forth between them. There isn't a resemblance that I can see. "Jack, is *everyone* in the Underground related to you in some way?"

Jack smiles. "Not quite everyone. Sorry, Celes, I should have introduced you. It's just that I haven't seen Uncle Jonas face to face since... well, I don't know how long it has been."

"You were eight," the other man supplies.

"Jonas is my mother's stepbrother," Jack explains. "We're not related by blood, but..."

"But sometimes you don't have to be," Jonas finishes for him. "We've kept in touch through messages over the years, and I've tried to keep an eye on Jack's career for Jacqueline's sake."

Jack nods. "Uncle Jonas, this is Celes."

Jonas extends a hand to me, and I take it. His grip is firm, but measured. His gaze is slightly more disconcerting. He looks at me closely, as though he's trying to spot something about me.

"Do I have something in my eye, or something?"

Jonas laughs. "No, sorry. It's just that... well, you don't know how excited I am to finally meet someone like you. Someone like Jacqueline was."

That's enough to make me feel a little strange. I know that the whole Underground thinks of me as special. I know that I have special powers. It's just something else to meet someone who is that obviously interested in what I am.

"Sorry," Jonas says. "I'm making you uncomfortable, aren't I?"

"Just a little bit," I reply.

"It's just quite an exciting day. I get to see Jack again after all these years, plus I get to meet you.

Jacqueline... well, I always knew that Jack's mother was special, but Sebastian and I only found out quite how special when she died, by which time it was too late to learn more directly."

"That didn't stop Sebastian trying," I say, remembering how interested the Location Six leader was in me.

"No, it didn't," Jonas agrees. "Sebastian got a little obsessed after Jacqueline's death, and I have to admit that I wasn't much better. It's... well, you can imagine how important some of the implications are. You're very special, Celes."

I shrug, still not entirely happy with that way of thinking. Not happy with some of the situations being what I am has put me in, either. "So far," I say, "being special has gotten me shot at, forced me to change my identity, and given me a power that means I kill people."

"But it's so much more than that," Jonas insists. "That's why I went along with Sebastian, trying to find others like Jacqueline. Like you. It's not just that Jacqueline was my sister, it's that her existence shows that there is more to the universe than just humanity. Than just Earth.

The whole parameters of our thoughts have to change to take that in."

Jack moves me gently away from Jonas a little. His uncle doesn't seem to take any offense at it.

"And now, of course, Jack has found you. I had started to worry that perhaps he was all that was left. That he was the last, lonely remnant of... well, whatever you both are. Which we will of course be able to find out far more about, now that Jack has brought us the rock for analysis."

So Jack has brought the rock over with him. I wonder how he managed to persuade Lionel to do that. Or maybe he didn't tell him. I have to say that, in spite of his over-eagerness, I quite like Jonas. There's something about him that's almost infectiously warm and curious. It reminds me a bit of my little brother, but it's more than that. I like the warmth Jack has towards his uncle. It's a total contrast to the stiff formality of his relationship with his father, and it makes me wonder how they got so close when they've met so little.

"I'm pleased to meet you, Jonas," I say. "I hope I can do something that will help with your research. I'd like to know where I come from as much as you do."

That makes Jonas grin, and he moves forward to pull me into a bear hug. "You know, you remind me of Jacqueline. She was so much the same as you, even down to her smile. And it's good to see Jack happy for once too. Even over his video messages, I've been able to spot the rosy glow of love, you know. You two are obviously made for one another."

I pull back. I get the feeling Jonas could be a bit intense in anything more than short bursts. Maybe that's why he's out here on his farm, away from the rest of the Underground. Still I can't help liking the compliment. Jack and I *are* perfect together. At least, I think so, and I want to keep things that way.

Jack rolled his eyes. "Ah, Jonas, it's time to get together with Lancaster and go through the final preparations. The Fortress of the Others is something else, and we all have to be prepared."

TWELVE

It's dark by the time we finally make our move on the Others' compound. I guess that makes sense. Darkness means an easier time of sneaking in, not to mention fewer people around who might potentially cause problems. That's important, because this is meant to be a rescue mission, not an all-out assault. Even so, I'm under no illusions about the danger we might be walking into. Jack makes me wear a flak jacket before he agrees to let me come, and gives me a pistol for self-defense. It has a silencer, which makes me feel like an extra out of a spy movie, but also serves to drive home just how dangerous the situation we're walking into is.

Of course, if that hadn't, then the sight of the Others' base would have. It's a big, ugly, windowless building three stories tall, sitting behind enough barbed wire to make it clear that no one sensible would want to go near it. There are armed guards patrolling the perimeter with dogs. I'm not sure how we're going to get past them as I crouch at the top of a small rise not far from the compound, along with Jack, Grayson, and the others involved in the rescue.

What surprises me is how close this place is to ordinary homes and houses. It's less than a mile from the heart of suburbia, yet it even *looks* like a secret base.

"I thought you said that the Others disguised their bases better than this," I say to Jack, keeping my voice low.

"Normally, they do," he whispers back. "The Fortress is a special case."

"The Fortress," Lionel puts in, moving closer almost silently, "is one of their most secure locations. We didn't know where it was until now."

I look down at the place below us in surprise. "How could you not spot *this*?"

"It could have been anywhere in the world," Jack points out. "Besides, it might not look like a house or a business, but if you didn't know what it was, wouldn't it just look like a secure warehouse? Or maybe something run by the government?"

"But wouldn't a government facility have signs outside, telling you what it is?" I ask.

Beside me, Lionel laughs softly, "You obviously haven't worked at the same ones I did, dear. Now, enough talking, we go on Jack's signal."

Jack talks into a radio ear piece. "Everybody ready?"

Voices come back, saying yes, one by one. Everybody around me looks ready. I'm easily the least heavily armed of the group around me. Everyone else has either a submachine-gun or some kind of elaborately modified rifle. Everything has sound suppressors fitted. Additionally, most of the people there have backpacks, undoubtedly containing a whole host of extra gear.

"Then we go in three, two, one. Go!"

The sentries and their dogs fall almost simultaneously. I look at Jack questioningly.

"Tranquilizer darts," he explains, "now come on."

We run for the fence as quickly and quietly as we can. The fence is electrified, but it isn't a problem, apparently. Jack says something else into his radio, and in the distance, I see half the lights in the area go out. The Underground has cut the power, I realize. Even while I'm thinking it, Lionel and Grayson move up to the fence, hacking a hole in it at lightning speed. In a matter of seconds, there's a gap big enough to walk through.

"Just in time," Jack says. "The emergency power will be on in a moment."

"Do you think they know that we're here yet?" Lionel asks.

"They would have to be very stupid not to, but we'll take precautions anyway."

Jack signals to another of the Faders, who brings forward a computer. The Fader taps in a series of commands before looking around at Jack. "I'm in their camera feeds now. I'll only be able to freeze a few at a time, but I should be able to mask your movements."

Jack nods. "That's good enough."

We move to a door, looking around for potential threats. I spot someone moving out of the shadows, gun raised, but as fast as I react, Jack is faster. He brings up his submachine gun, and gets a silenced shot off in the dark. The figure falls. No one comments.

The doors to the Fortress go with its name. From a distance, they don't look like much, just ordinary loading doors to let trucks drive in, the way people would have at just about any warehouse. Closer too, though, I can see that they're reinforced steel. There's a retinal scan lock similar to the ones back at the Underground base.

"Time to see if this works," Jack says. He takes a small box from his backpack, opens it, and then presses something to each of his eyes in turn. I realize that he's putting in contact lenses. He bends over the scanner, and a light goes green, before those great metal doors slide open in near silence.

The Faders move through them, checking the space beyond. This is obviously the most dangerous point of the mission. Even I would want to ambush us here, and I don't know anything about military tactics. Jack and Grayson, who obviously know far more, stay by the doors until we get the all clear to move in further.

The room beyond is some kind of loading bay, and we get out of it quickly, leaving a couple of Faders behind to keep our escape route secure. We move deeper into the Fortress, following corridors that have no signs beyond a few stenciled numbers and letters. Presumably, the Others know what they mean, but we don't. We're left trying to find our way around the base by trial and error.

It's a total maze. If Location Six was confusing because of the amount of things that had to be fit into it, this feels like it is almost deliberately so, with corridors taking twists and turns for no apparent reason, while doors lead off at the sides at random intervals. We have to check each one we come to, just to make sure that we aren't leaving a whole bunch of potential enemies behind us. For the most part, there isn't anybody there.

That changes quickly when we round a corner and almost run straight into a guard in the Others' traditional black clothing. Jack reacts before any of the rest of us, spinning him around and putting him in a choke hold that has the guard slumping into unconsciousness in a matter of seconds. It's quick, it's quiet, and it has me wondering what I'm doing there. I can't keep up with that kind of thing.

The guard isn't the only person we run into. A little further on, we find a lab, with toughened glass windows facing out onto the corridor, and plenty of expensive looking pieces of machinery inside. There's also a woman in a white coat bent over a microscope, apparently making notes as she works. She appears to be in her mid-twenties, with long blonde hair tied carefully back and glasses. Jack starts to open the door to the lab. What is he planning?

Jack moves quickly over to the woman, putting his gun to her head. "If you call for help or reach for a weapon, you're dead, understood?"

The woman freezes in place. "I... I..."

She's panicking. She's going to try something stupid, like screaming. I know I have to do something, so I move forward, level with her. "What's your name?" I ask.

"Teri. Oh God, please don't kill me."

"We aren't going to kill you," I promise her. I hope that's true. I know how much the Underground hates the Others. "We need information, Teri. We need you to tell us where Sebastian Cook is being held."

Teri shakes her head. "I don't know any Sebastian Cook."

"Don't lie," Jack warns. His voice is cold enough to be terrifying. But then, I guess that's the point.

"I'm not lying," Teri says. She starts to look around, but thinks better of it. "I'm not. I swear."

"Where would they take important prisoners, Teri?" I ask.

She swallows. "The top floor. The northern corner. There are... cells there. There's one... the glass cell. If he's important, he might be in there."

"Thank you," I say, looking at Jack. Thankfully, he understands what I want, which is for him not to go around shooting frightened young scientists. We leave Teri tied up, and head upstairs in search of Jack's father. We're moving quickly now, so when we run into a guard post with half a dozen armed men, there almost isn't time to react.

Almost. Jack presses me flat against the wall, firing off a burst from his weapon one handed. Lionel fires almost as quickly, while Gray and the others follow suit. In less than a couple of seconds, the danger is gone. It's only in the aftermath that I see the steel door beyond them, complete with another electronic lock, which Jack sets about breaking through as smoothly as we got through the first.

The room beyond is larger than I thought it would be. It's a big, steel walled square, with a glass cube inside it. Sebastian sits inside that cube, on the floor. He doesn't appear to have been harmed, but he's clearly a prisoner there, and he doesn't react when we approach.

"The cube will be one way glass," Lionel says. "It's an effective way of cutting someone off from the world." He goes to the door. There's a lock on the outside, and the retired major takes a more direct approach to it than Jack. He smashes it with the butt of his gun, before flinging the door open. We move through into the cube. From inside, the walls are opaque. They remind me of the glass back in the viewing room of Location Six.

"Hello, Sebastian," Lionel says. "Welcome to the escape attempt."

Sebastian stands, smiling weakly. "Just like Kuala Lumpur."

"I hope not," Lionel replies. "I got shot on that one, if you remember."

A voice comes over hidden speakers. A voice I recognize all too well. A voice that means that things have just become a lot more dangerous than they were. "And you could still get shot on this one, Sir Lionel."

The glass goes from cloudy to clear in a matter of seconds, revealing a group of the Others surrounding the cell. They're as heavily armed as the Faders are, and at their head is Richard, Grayson's father. He stands there casually, as if he hasn't just set up a huge stand-off. It's not him I'm looking at though. I'm looking at the three figures next to him, all standing with their hands handcuffed behind their backs, looking like they have no clue what's going on.

"Mom, Dad? Bailey?"

My family looks at me without recognition. Of course they do. They've been Faded. I remember them, but they have no recollection of my ever existing.

"Put your weapons down," Richard instructs. "Do it now, or I don't need to tell you what will happen."

I see Jack wince slightly. Grayson, however, does more than wince.

"It isn't enough you used your own son to get to Celes, Dad?" he snaps. "Now you're using innocent civilians who don't even know what this is all about? You disgust me."

THIRTEEN

Richard actually looks a little sad as Grayson steps forward to berate him. Maybe he wasn't expecting it. Maybe it's just the betrayal of it, his own son siding with the Underground. The Others don't open fire though. I guess that's partly because of the walls of the glass cube, which, if they're anything like those back at the Underground will be tougher than they look, but maybe it's also because Richard doesn't want his son hurt.

"You know," Sebastian says, moving to back Grayson up and nodding towards my family through the glass walls of the room. "You've really crossed the line here, Richard, bringing in innocent civilians like this. These people don't even know why they're here."

Richard shakes his head. Beside him, my family stand still, guarded closely by a trio of the Others, all with guns trained on them. "They know," he says. "And they're part of this. They're with Celestra Caine."

"Really?" Sebastian asks, without raising his voice. He looks over to where Bailey stands and points at me. "You, young man, do you know who this young woman is?"

Bailey looks nervous. He would. He's surrounded by armed people, in a situation he knows nothing about. I'm almost proud of him when he manages to shake his head. Proud, and a little sad. I've known in theory that my family won't remember me, but seeing the truth of it like this is something different. It hurts, even though I know that right now, it could be the thing that keeps Bailey safe. If there's no connection to me, then there's no leverage. There's no reason to want to kill them, if that won't have any effect on me.

"What about you two?" Sebastian asks, looking at my parents now. They seem as blank as Bailey was. "Do you remember her?"

"Of course they do," Richard snaps, not giving them a chance to answer. "She's their daughter. They raised her for seventeen years. They know everything about her."

It's my father who answers. "Sorry, I don't know who you think we are, but…"

"You're her parents. She is your daughter."

"We don't have a daughter," my mother says, and it's heartbreaking now, even as I know that she isn't doing it to hurt me. She simply doesn't remember, but that's what hurts. "I don't think we've even met this girl before."

I want to cry, but I know I can't. If I cry, it will show how much they mean to me. If I cry, it will show the Others that what they're doing is working. Grayson moves to put an arm around my shoulders for comfort. Jack doesn't move, but then, he probably gets how important it is to minimize the connection between me and my family right now. He's also busily watching the Others, readying himself for the fight he knows must be coming.

I try not to think about that fight. The Underground's Faders have plenty of guns, but so do the Others, and they have us surrounded out in the open, where they could potentially cut us down with a burst of bullets. There isn't much cover for them, either. Any battle now is going to be a bloody one, and a lot of people are going to die on both sides. Maybe that's why no one has given the order to fire yet.

Richard shrugs then. "It doesn't matter if they remember her or not, just as long as she remembers them. You don't want to see your family hurt, do you, Celestra?"

I know what I have to do. I have to protect my family in the only way that they can be protected right now. I have to play the part I was meant to play. I have to be the person the Underground tried to Fade me into being, before they realized that it wouldn't work. "Celestra? My name is Celeste. Who are these people? Why have you brought them out here?"

Richard looks amused, and I know that my act hasn't even begun to fool him. He's too clever to be taken in. Or maybe he's simply not willing to believe that the situation wouldn't work out the way he wants it to. "You grew up with them, Celestra. Even Grayson remembers them, so there's no point in you trying to lie your way out of this. They're your family. The only family you've known. Now, persuade your friends to put their weapons down, or they die."

"And then what, Richard?" Sebastian asks. He doesn't seem very bothered by the prospect. "We have a gun battle?"

That's what I've been worried will happen, but Sebastian says it like it isn't any kind of threat at all.

"Do you want things to get that far?" Richard demands. "Do you want some kind of glorious last stand?"

Sebastian smiles. "I don't think that will work. I take it you used the compound you came up with for these walls? You know, the bulletproof one?"

"Do you want to find out the hard way?" Richard asks. "Are you willing to bet your life that our weapons won't get through it?"

Beside me, Sebastian's smile just widens. "I've always had a lot of faith in your skills as a scientist, Richard, if not in your capabilities as a human being."

"You're trying to lecture me on morals?" Richard demands.

Sebastian shrugs. "Well, I'm not the one threatening to kill three civilians."

"No," Richard says, "you aren't. Which is why you'll put your weapons down and come out, before I decide to start killing them."

That gets another burst of anger from Grayson. "Dad," he says. "How can you? We went on family trips with the Caines, we had family parties, celebrated birthdays together. We've known them for years. Does it boil down to this? You threatening them? Why do you hate Celes so much that you're doing this? What did she ever do to you?"

Richard shakes his head, looking momentarily angry. He starts to gesture towards the Others holding my family, but then stops. "Stay out of this, Grayson."

"How can I?" Grayson looks around at me, then at the glass-walled room we're in. "I'm in here just as much as anyone else, and it's Celes you're trying to hurt. I'm not going to let you do that."

Richard glares at Sebastian. His voice, when it comes, is tight with anger. "This is your doing, isn't it, old friend? Taking my son and twisting his mind. Turning him against me, so that he thinks I'm the one doing something wrong. That's what you do, after all, isn't it? That's what you always did, even with your own family. You pretend that you're helping people, but all you ever do is hurt them. You control their minds, change their lives, and play God, as though you have any *clue* about what's best for them."

"You were happy enough to help me at the start, Richard," Sebastian says, still apparently unconcerned by what's going on around us. "You worked with me on the original operations. You even helped me to set up many of the protocols I used."

"And then I learned better," Richard shoots back. It's obvious that this is about more than just the Others and the Underground. Or maybe it's at the *heart* of that rivalry. After all, the two men are very high up in their organizations. Maybe those organizations wouldn't exist without whatever's between the two of them.

Grayson asks what we're all wondering. "Dad, what happened? Whatever it was, it can't be enough to justify you hurting people like the Caines. Let them go. They don't know anything. They shouldn't be part of this."

"*You* shouldn't be part of it," Richard says. "Yet they've taken you and twisted you, until you aren't even my son anymore. Can they put you back to the way you were? Can they give you your old memories back?"

"Dad..."

"And what about my family?"

"Grayson's your family," I point out.

"Not my first family." Richard sounds furious now. "Not the wife and daughter your Underground friends took from me, making it so that they didn't remember me. So that I didn't remember them. I married Grayson's mother when he was just a toddler, not knowing any better."

"You're my stepdad?" Grey asks. "But I always thought-"

"You were a toddler when I married your mother, but I raised you as my own," Richard says. "You were my son, until Sebastian twisted you."

"I'm still your son," Grayson says, "and I don't think you'll let your friends shoot me." He steps out of the glass walled cell, raising his gun to point it at his father. "But that doesn't mean I can't shoot you. Mr. and Mrs. Caine, Bailey, go over to my friends now."

My family look confused, but they start to move. A couple of the Others start to intercept them.

"Stay back or he dies," Grayson promises.

Richard sighs. "Haven't we been here before, Grayson?"

He moves, trying to grab the gun from his son, but Grayson kicks his feet out from under him, pressing the gun tighter to his father's head. "Yes, we have, and you caved in that time, too. Now, if your people don't put their weapons down, then I will shoot you." Grayson reached down to pull Richard's head back, so that the gun was pressed beneath his chin.

Richard looks frightened. Frightened, but also angry that his son should be doing this. "You don't even remember who I am, do you?"

"I remember," Grayson says.

"No, you don't. Not really. You wouldn't be able to do this if you really remembered. Sebastian has messed with your head so much that you think I'm the enemy, rather than him and the crooks who work with him."

"Shut up," Gray says, pushing the gun harder into his father. "When you went after Celes, ready to kill her, when you used me to get to her, *that's* when you became my enemy. This... all of this just confirms it. You're evil. You need to be stopped."

Down on his knees, Richard shrugs. "Then stop me."

"I will if you don't tell your men to drop their weapons."

Richard shakes his head once more. "We went through this the last time you put a gun to my head, son. I am not commanding my men to stop."

"Then I will," Grayson says, looking around at the assembled Others. "You might not care what happens to you, but they will. You're too senior for them to risk. Now, all of you, do you want to get him killed? No? Then drop your weapons."

They hesitate only briefly, before the first rifle clatters to the ground. More follow. Soon, the Others are unarmed, while the Faders have snatched up their weapons again, moving out from the cell to take the weapons the Others had away from them.

FOURTEEN

"Now what?" Richard demands, once his followers have been disarmed. "Are you going to kill us? It's what the Underground and the Others do when they meet, isn't it? Fight to the death."

"Don't tempt me," Jack says, but he's looking at me as he says it, and I know he isn't going to kill anyone. Even Sebastian seems to concur on that point.

"Take their means of communication away and lock them in my cell," the Underground leader says. "It should hold them until we are all well clear of this compound."

The Underground's Faders rush to do as he orders, taking away radios and phones from the Others before herding them into the glass cube. With the lock damaged, the best they can manage is to wedge it shut, but it looks like it should be solid. Besides, there's still the outer door to lock as well.

I go over to my family. They look frightened and confused, even when Jack comes over to let them out of the handcuffs holding them. They look at me suspiciously, as though they aren't sure what to think about me.

My mother speaks. "They said before that you were... that you're our..."

"That doesn't matter right now," I say, trying to be firm so that she doesn't see how I really feel in that moment. I can't go back. I know that. It's better just to pretend like I never existed, because for them at least, I never did.

"But who are you?" my father asks.

I shake my head. "That doesn't matter either. What matters is that we're going to get you out of here."

"Celes here has a point," Lionel says, moving over to the door to the room and peeking out. "We should be going. Everybody form up on me. The Caines and Celes should stay close to Jack. You too, Sebastian, at least until we can get you armed."

Sebastian picks up one of the Others' guns. It's a bulky combat rifle that seems at odds with the man holding it. "There, is that better?"

"Except for the parts where you aren't wearing body armor, you've only recently escaped captivity, and you aren't much of a shot at the best of times?" Lionel asks.

"Aside from that."

"Then everything is fine. Come on. Or were we going to stay until every enemy in the Fortress shows up?"

We get moving, hurrying after Lionel. Jack sticks close to his father, near the front of the group, obviously intent on keeping him from harm. Grayson stays close to my family, presumably to help protect them. No, I realize, not just for that. He's staying close because he's a face they know and trust, whereas everyone else, including me, is just some heavily armed stranger. It's enough to make me push closer to the front, not wanting the pain that comes every time their eyes skim over me without the faintest hint of recognition.

That's why I'm there when Jack comes skidding to a halt, grabbing Lionel and yanking him back almost quickly enough to send everyone else crashing into him. I only just stop in time as he kneels, hand raised for us to hold our positions.

"What is it?" the major asks.

Jack nods to the floor. Or, more accurately, to a space about six inches above it. He takes something from his bag, an aerosol spray of some kind, and sprays it, revealing a series of crisscrossing red beams of light.

"Alarms," he says.

"They weren't here when we came in," Lionel observes.

Sebastian steps up for a closer look. "Well, they're here now. Richard must have turned them on as he came in after us. If I know him, they'll be wired up to the lockdown sequences for the building. Trigger the alarm, and we'll quickly find ourselves trapped."

That doesn't sound good. Particularly not with a whole group of angry Others operatives just a few hallways back from us. "Can we disarm it?" I ask.

Jack nods. "If I can get to the control panel, at least."

"And that is..."

Jack points to the other end of the hall, beyond the beams, and I can just make out a small panel on the wall. "Everybody else, wait here."

It's hard to watch as Jack tiptoes his way through the beams. It's not just that he could hit one at any second, though I know he could, even though he was somehow able to pick up on the danger presented by the beams before. It's also how far in front of the rest of us he has to go. If one of the Others were to come in now, he'd be incredibly vulnerable.

A guard rounds the corner at the far end of the hall. I go to shout a warning to Jack, but I know it's already too late. There's nothing I can do as the guard starts to raise his...

Pfft.

I can't place the sudden noise until the guard falls back, dead, and I look around to see Lionel lowering his silenced rifle. It's an impressive shot. A *very* impressive shot.

"Just like being back in... well, never mind."

Jack makes it to the end of the hall, and it turns out that the guard has a key card for the alarms. Jack uses it, and we're able to move on, trying to make up lost time. At least, we hurry until Sebastian stops outside one of the Fortress's many doors.

"What are you doing?" Jack asks. "We don't have time to stop."

"We're in the heart of one of the Others' key operations," Sebastian says. "Some of their biggest secrets are in this building, and this might be the only chance we get to uncover them."

"It's also a chance to get us all killed," Jack retorts. "This is meant to be a rescue. We have Celes'… the Caines to think of."

"We have the whole future of the planet to think of," Sebastian says, and reaches for the door handle.

Jack's eyes widen. "Wait!"

For once, he's not quick enough to stop what is about to happen. Sebastian tries the door handle, it turns just a fraction, and then an alarm sounds. It's piercing. It's shrill. Worse than that, If Sebastian was correct before, it means that the whole place is about to go into lockdown.

Lionel takes one look at Sebastian, shakes his head, and bellows back at the rest of the Faders. "Run! Everybody run! Now, unless you want to be stuck here!"

He sprints for the next junction of corridors, and the Faders jerk into action, taking off after him. Grayson pulls my mother and father into motion, while Jack grabs Bailey, forcing him to keep up. I run with them, confident thanks to the part of me that isn't human that I can easily move quickly enough, yet unwilling to leave them behind. Even if they can't remember me, I can remember them.

The Fortress is starting to wake up, its inhabitants roused by the alarms and stumbling out bleary eyed into corridors. Jack shoots a guard who comes out of the wrong door, while Lionel takes down another with a blow from the butt of his rifle.

The alarm starts to be accompanied by an automated voice as we run. "Base lockdown initiated," it says. "All personnel, please remain in your designated safe areas."

We don't have much time left, from the sound of it. A scientist moves out in front of us, slowing us down for less than a second before Jack smashes him aside. More guards rush out, but Jack and Lionel shoot them on the run. Lionel isn't as fast as Jack, but he doesn't move like an old man by any means.

Lights start to come on above doors around us, and I hear the loud snap of locks engaging, but that doesn't affect us. We're just trying to get out of the building. We run back through to the loading area at the front of the place, where the great steel doors that opened to let us in are. There are a couple more guards there, but they don't last any longer than the others we have run into in the course of our rush to escape. Though the sound of shouting somewhere behind us suggests that they will be along in greater numbers soon. We have to be out of the building by then.

That should be easy, except that the doors in front of us are starting to swing shut. By the time we're out onto the main floor level of the loading bay, they're more than halfway closed.

"Quick," Lionel says, "everybody through."

As if to underline the urgency, he sprints through the gap. Sebastian does the same, along with the first few Faders. Jack looks back at me, and I look back at my family.

"I'll get them out," Jack says.

"But Jack..."

I don't get the chance to argue. He shoves me bodily through the closing gap in the doors. I stumble and fall outside, hitting the dirt hard and rolling so that I'm looking back at that ever closing gap. Faders come through it, hurrying even more now as their opportunity for escape literally starts to disappear before their eyes.

Grayson appears, pulling Bailey through. I mouth a silent thank you to him as my mother and father follow, pushed through by Jack. The doors are closing tighter now, so that there's barely room for someone to squeeze through.

"Jack," I call back, "hurry up."

Jack leaps through the gap, making it through easily, and a final couple of Faders try to follow him. The first makes it, barely. The second, an older Fader who I'm sure must be one of the instructors from Location Two… the second isn't so lucky. The great steel doors slam shut on his leg as he tries to throw himself through, clamping shut like the limb between them is nothing and slicing it above the knee. The man screams. I'd never thought that someone could scream like that. I start to move to help him, but he passes out. I reach down to try and pull him clear of the doors, but Jack pulls me away from him.

"There's nothing we can do for him," he says. "If you move him, he'll bleed out in seconds. I know it's hard, but we need to keep moving."

I force myself to nod. I know he's right. The man behind us has given his life trying to get Sebastian and my family to safety, I won't dishonor that effort by wasting the time that we have to get away. I turn to make the run back to the cars through the surrounding darkness, and that's when I see lights come on towards the perimeter of the compound. By those lights, I can just make out a dozen or so men in black combat armor, carrying very intimidating looking assault weapons.

"Oh dear," Lionel says from the front, hefting his rifle, "it seems that we've kicked a hornet's nest here. Do those look like elite troops to anyone else?"

"They're not that elite if they light themselves up neatly rather than ambushing us in the dark," one of the Faders points out. Then he dies, shot from the side, away from the group under the lights. They're nothing but a distraction. We're under attack!

FIFTEEN

Grayson pushes my family to the ground as bullets fly past us, and suddenly, it's like I'm in the middle of a war zone. The Others come at us from all sides, and for cover, we only have the buildings around us. I try to stay near my family. I know they don't remember who I am, but I'm going to keep them safe, no matter what it takes.

The Faders around me react in different ways. A couple of the ones from Location Six panic, firing blindly. It just makes them targets for the gunfire coming our way, and they're quickly brought down by bullets. Jack and the rest work on getting low, finding what cover they can before firing back. Jack fires in his customary careful bursts, always seeming to know exactly where the danger is coming from. A little way from him, Lionel has managed to scramble onto the roof of one of the compound's outbuildings, letting him pick people off with that rifle of his.

One of the Others comes into view, heading for us with his gun raised. I react on instinct, firing off two shots with the pistol Jack gave me, and he falls back. In the darkness, I don't know if I have killed him or not. Right then, I'm too busy worrying about where the next threat will come from to even think about that.

There's an almighty bang and a blinding flash of light then, and a second after, I find that two of the Others have a grip on my arms as they move in close behind their flash grenade. Grayson, who's just a feet away, charges forward even though his own ears must still be ringing. He kicks one of the Others viciously, whirling away as the second tries to go for his gun, releasing me in the process. Grayson goes into him hard, throwing punches and knees that don't give his opponent time to react. He forces the man back long enough that Grayson can clear his weapon, and two shots later, the fight is over.

"Thanks," I say, but Grayson is already moving again, rejoining the fight. He fights well now, and I guess those lessons with the Fader instructors must have done something, though there are plenty of other people there who can fight better. Jack, for one. He isn't even affected by the flash grenade, and I realize it's because he had the foresight to move back from it even as it landed. His whole fighting style is like that. It's like he knows exactly what each of his opponents is going to do before they do it, so that he's always ready, turning to face them with his gun ready to fire, or meeting them with a quick attack as they come in.

Lionel's down from the roof now, and he pauses just long enough to throw one of the Others to the ground before waving over at us.

"We need to fight our way clear. Make for the vehicles."

He's right, of course. We can't stay there. We scramble for the gap we made in the fence, and I herd my family towards it. Sebastian helps, which makes me think a little better of him, though I guess it's just because he doesn't want them slowing us down. Behind us, the fight goes on. I see Others and Faders struggling, and it's hard to tell who is winning, though I worry about our side. Some of the Faders from Location Six have minor injuries, while the instructors from Location Two can't have been on a live operation recently. Even though they seem to be holding their own for the moment, this was never meant to be a full scale battle situation.

All I can do for the moment though is run, moving from cover to cover within the compound, trying to make sure that my family aren't out in the open for long enough for the Others to shoot at them. Whenever shots come close, I fire back, not trying to hit anything so much as simply persuade the person firing to duck back into cover long enough for us to move.

Jack is much more precise, and several times I see his shots hit. Lionel fights efficiently, calmly, marshaling the Faders around us even as he continues to target the elite of the Others. One of those men rushes at him, and Lionel ducks low, sending him sprawling over him.

We make it to the section of fence we've taken out, but there's a problem. The power is back on now, so anyone going through it will have to be careful. So careful that they will make a perfect target for the Others as they fire back at us. Yet we need to get through it, because that's the only way back to the cars.

Jack, Lionel, and those Faders who aren't injured, turn back towards the Others, forming a wall of shooters. I realize that their plan is to counterattack and draw fire while people escape. It seems suicidal. That close together, they're a natural target. There has to be another way. Only I can't see what that other way might be.

Grayson is the first through the fence, making sure that there are no surprises on that side of it, while Sebastian follows him. My family are next, moving through the electrified fence one by one, all looking terrified as they do it. Grayson guides them up the slope towards the waiting cars.

"You're next, Celes," Jack calls back, firing a burst at the Others to keep them occupied. In that moment, I'm terrified. Not of the fence, though I guess I should be scared about the prospect of thousands of volts running through me if I so much as slip. No, I'm scared because this seems far too similar to the way I left Location Six, abandoning Jack to take the helicopter, leaving him to his fate.

"No," I say, "I'm not going anywhere until you do."

"Celes," Jack yells back, "there isn't time to argue. You're far too important to risk losing."

"And you aren't?" I demand. I fire back at the Others, moving up alongside Jack. At that point though, Lionel falls back, clutching his leg. I realize he's been shot. It doesn't so much as slow him down, though. All it means is that he has to roll onto his belly to keep shooting. He's an extremely tough old man.

"Get her out of here, Jack," he orders, and Jack nods. He takes me by the arm, pulling me back to the fence.

"Looks like you're coming with me after all," I say.

He kisses me, so briefly that the brush of lips is barely there. "Only as far as the car. Then I'm coming back to give Lionel and the rest covering fire from the top of the slope."

I want to argue, to tell him that it's too dangerous, but I know that there isn't time to spend arguing, at least until we get to the cars. Jack and I run up the slope, making it to the top with that strange speed we both have.

It's then that a trio of Others jump out at us.

Jack is already turning as they attack, bringing his gun to bear, but for once, I'm faster. I reach out for one of them, and the power within me leaps up, arcing out into him to incinerate him as I touch him. It's quick; even quicker than it was the last time I did this to someone. One moment he's there, the next, there isn't even a body, the power within me has burned so hot. It's like the force I had before, only multiplied tenfold.

The second of them starts to raise a gun, and I laugh. I don't know why I laugh, except that it seems ludicrous that this human should try something so obviously useless. I grab the gun, and he screams as it melts in his hand. I grab his arm and the moment when his body vaporizes is almost peaceful. After all, it's not like there's time for his mind to register the pain of it before there's nothing left of him.

Jack deals with the third one, grabbing him and throwing him down the slope to crash into the fence. There's a flash as the electricity does its job, but it's almost disappointing that Jack didn't give him to me. Didn't let me flow through him in his final instants.

Jack looks different to these eyes, glowing with power. More… just *more*, as though there are whole dimensions to him that I don't normally get to see. I reach out to him, even as some part of me inside screams at me not to touch him. I ignore it. What does it know? I take Jack in my arms, and I kiss him, sharing the power of what I am, running it through him, letting him feel it. I have to be careful; after all, there is still far too much human about him, but I do it. I do it until he glows like me.

"Do you understand yet?" I ask as I pull back from him.

"I... Celes..."

As it has done before, the name pulls me back to myself, and I'm left standing there as both Jack and I cease to glow.

"Jack, what..."

"It's all right, Celes. It's fine."

I shake my head. "It's getting stronger. I can feel it."

Jack shushes me, holding me close. "We need to get you into the car now, Celes."

"What about Lionel?"

I look back, and a few more Faders are coming up the hill, having made it through the fence. There's still plenty more back in the compound though.

Jack touches his ear piece. "Lionel, Celes and I have made it to the top of the hill. I'm in position to give you covering fire while you get out."

There's no answer. Below, Lionel is busily firing at anything that comes out into the open.

"Major," Jack says, "can you read me?"

An irritated noise comes over the radio. "I'm reading you loud and clear. Which I shouldn't be. What are you still doing here, boy?"

"Like I said, I'm in position to give covering fire while..."

"Yes, yes. Only it doesn't work like that, Jack. You know it. I've been shot through the leg. How do you propose I get through that fence of yours? Hold on a moment." Below, Lionel's rifle fires, and one of the Others drops some distance away. "Got you."

"So we're just meant to abandon you?" Jack demands. "Isn't that just swapping one lot of hostages for another?"

"Oh, I don't imagine they'll take the likes of me hostage."

That isn't exactly an improvement, to my ears. Or to Jack's, apparently. "Major..."

"Oh, do shut up, boy. It's not like I've ever been one for goodbyes. Everybody here is too injured to make it, and they know it. Now, get a move on. I think there's more of them coming."

There are. I see the doors to the Fortress start to swing open, and Others pour out. I think I can vaguely make out Richard even at this distance.

"Celes," the major says over the radio, "do an old man a favor and get Jack out of here. Now, please."

He doesn't have to tell me twice. I take one last look at the approaching Others, grab hold of Jack, and run for the cars.

SIXTEEN

I can't answer Lionel, not looking at Jack as I am. I can see the hurt that the older man's sacrifice is about to do him written clearly on Jack's face. I reach out for him.

"We could go back. We could try to get him out as well. I'm willing to try it if you will."

Jack hesitates, and I can see that he wants to say yes, but he shakes his head. It seems that he isn't going to go against an order from Lionel. Isn't going to risk my safety.

"No," he says. "Lionel's right. We have to go. And he… he's going out a hero. Besides, he gave me an order."

"It's a good thing I don't have to listen to orders then," I say. I can still feel the remnants of the energy I used in fighting the others bubbling just below the surface, and I use it now. I use it to run, faster than Jack can move to stop me. I use it to reach out for the fence, ignoring the electricity in it. I touch it, and a whole section shorts out in a shower of sparks, falling down.

Others run at me. I reach out for them, touching them almost gently. The power within me rises up to incinerate them. There are more, struggling with Lionel hand to hand. The Faders with him are dead, leaving him as the last of them. The Others seem content for the moment to try to subdue him, but how long will it be before that changes? I don't know. I do know that I can feel the energy within me rising to the surface even more strongly as I see it. Lionel might not be Jack, but watching the old man die will hurt Jack too much to let it happen.

I run at the Others, and they see me coming, but it's too late for them. The first few of them can't run as I reach out to touch them one by one, making brief human candles of them. Even the next nearest few are not fast enough. I lunge after them, and they die too.

There are bullets then, flying around me as more of the Others turn their attention to me. There are bullets going the other way too, and I glance back to see Jack firing at those people targeting me. There's an old man too, one with a rifle of some kind. I wonder briefly if I should burn him too. He isn't one of us, after all. He isn't like me or Jack, and it would take so little to destroy him. So very...

No. I force myself to focus. I will not be overwhelmed by this. That's Lionel, I tell myself. Tell the part of me that seems so very inhuman. I'm trying to get him out. The glowing part of me doesn't really understand it, but it seems to know what I want. It even stops for long enough for me to be able to grab Lionel without hurting him.

"I'm sure I told you to leave me," he says.

"We need to go."

"And how do you propose I do that on this leg?"

In the end, I prop him up, and we limp along towards the fence together. I try not to think about the people behind us with guns, and not only because it's a frightening thought. There's a part of me that still wants to rush at them. That wants to burn them all. I have to fight to keep it from the surface.

Jack fires over our heads at the Others behind us, forcing them back. I keep hold of Lionel, more or less pushing him up the hill. I wonder if I would have had the strength to do that a year ago. Almost certainly not.

When we get closer to the top, Jack takes over from me, putting Lionel's arm around his shoulders to support him. The Others hang back, apparently unwilling to follow us closely, so we quickly make it to the cars intended as our escape. Grayson is in one of them with the engine running. The other cars have already gone.

"Hurry," he says. "The Caines and the rest of the Faders have gone on ahead, but we need to go, now."

We squeeze into the car. I barely have my door shut before Grayson hits the gas, driving as fast as he can through the darkness around us. For the first mile or so, he doesn't even bother with full lights, obviously trying to avoid attention from any of the Others who might come after us. He only relaxes back into normal driving once we're well clear of the Fortress, taking us back to the farm at what is still a decent pace, but one that isn't quite so breakneck.

Even with the speed we use in getting back, the rest of the Faders have beaten us there. We head into the farm house to find Faders having wounds bandaged, sitting around eating, and trying to make sense of exactly how the mission went. Sebastian is at one end of the room talking to Jonas. They look up as we come in with Lionel, and Jonas nods an acknowledgement. I guess, with all the Faders we lost, this isn't the time for anything more effusive.

Jack takes Lionel off to get medical attention. It's then that Sebastian starts to speak.

"I'd just like to thank everyone," he says, not loudly, but in the quiet aftermath of the mission, it carries through the room. "I know attacking the Fortress isn't something we've ever tried before, and I know it cost us some good friends. Thank you for taking that much of a risk. I'd like to believe that I'm able to make it worth it, because being a Fader should be about more than just what's best for a single person. I think everyone here lived up to that kind of higher standard tonight. And thanks to tonight's mission, we have seen more of something beyond the merely human."

He gestures towards me then, and the eyes of everyone in the room turn to me. They're quiet, and it occurs to me that every person here has seen what I can do. They've seen me glow with power. They've seen me kill. I don't know if I want that kind of attention. Not for that. Not for something that scares me more and more, because I'm starting to wonder if I really have any kind of control over it.

"Celestra is proof of what we have been fighting for all this time," Sebastian says. "There is life beyond what we see and know. There are things that we have yet to discover, and they can help us. All our efforts and our losses have not been in vain. We will continue to discover more. We will not let the Others stop us. Good job tonight everyone."

Sebastian's words do a lot to lift the subdued atmosphere of the room. I guess that, for the first time, the Faders are really seeing how much their efforts might achieve. Even though it feels to me like the whole mission went badly wrong, it probably still counts as a major coup for them.

It isn't long before Jack comes back from taking Lionel for treatment, I go up to him and he takes me into his arms.

"What's going to happen next?" I ask.

"What do you mean?"

"Everyone has seen what I've done, what I've become. They've seen what I really am. So what now, Jack?"

Jack nods. I know he understands the fear behind those words. After all, he has been hiding what he is from his friends for a long time. "You're safe," Jack promises.

"You saw tonight how far the Faders will go over this, and right now, you're the most valuable find we have."

"Well, that's one way to make me feel special. I'm a find now?"

Jack smiles, kissing me. "You know what I mean."

"So I'm safe?"

"You are here, though don't be surprised if people look at you a little differently. Just because you're what everyone here has been looking for all these years, that doesn't mean you aren't strange to them. They don't know you yet."

"I'm not that strange," I point out. "You're like me, and they know you."

"But they don't know that. I'm not sure they'd even believe me if I were to tell them." Jack looks around the room. No one seems to be looking at us. "I'm just Jack to them now, and unless they saw me glowing, that wouldn't change."

Which they didn't. I glowed in public. I disintegrated people. Jack... well, like he said, he was just Jack.

"I don't even think I should tell them right now," Jack says.

I don't get that. Is Jack ashamed of what he is? Is he ashamed of being like me?

"Why not?" I demand.

"Only a few people know, right now," Jack says. "My father, Jonas, Lionel. Not the other Faders. They would think of all the years I lied to them, and it would cause problems. Then there's how they would be on assignments. They wouldn't know whether to protect me or let me do my job. I'd be something to be studied, not the guy who could get them out of trouble."

"How do you think I feel," I ask, "with everybody trying to protect me? After all, who rescued Lionel back there?"

Jack smiles at that, kissing me again. "Thank you for that, Celes, but next time, please don't take that risk. Lionel had already given an order for us to go."

"Since when do you care about orders?"

"It's not just that," Jack says. "In a situation like that, if you go back, other people will go back with you, and that could get them hurt. Sometimes, it's about weighing up the consequences."

I shake my head. "What's the point in weighing up consequences if it means you end up doing something you know isn't right? I couldn't just leave Lionel behind, Jack, not with what it would have done to you."

"And if it had just been the other Faders?" Jack asks. "The ones who died?"

I don't answer him, because I don't have an answer. Would I have left them behind? I almost left Lionel, getting as far as the cars before going back. So I can't say that I definitely would have gone back to try to help them. The part of me I can't control certainly wasn't thinking that way. It was thinking about Jack. It was thinking about how he would be hurt if Lionel died.

It was thinking about the opportunity to hurt more of the Others. I don't want to think about that, but I can't avoid it. The part of me that is getting more powerful is also getting more dangerous. How close did I come to killing Lionel in those moments before I remembered who he was?

I shake my head. "Can't we just enjoy the moment, Jack? Your father's free. Lionel's safe, and I... well, I have my family back for a little while too. I'm not sure that the rest matters very much."

SEVENTEEN

"You should go see your family." Jack suggests. "They're just in the next room."

I shake my head. It's not that I don't want to. I do. I can just picture them there, trying to make sense of everything, drinking coffee brought to them by one of the Faders. But I'm scared. Scared of what it will be like.

"They don't know me anymore, Jack," I say. "I'm not sure I can sit there with them, knowing everything about them, when they haven't even got a clue who I might be."

Jack shrugs. "It's your decision, but I know I'd want to see them, Celes."

I don't answer that immediately. "What will happen to them now?"

Jack lets that deflection go. Why is he so kind to me? "The Others obviously know about their cover identities here," he says. "And there's no reason to suggest that they will stop being a threat. If anything, they'll be more of a problem now that they've seen you in action at their base."

Jack doesn't have to spell out the implications of that. "It isn't safe for them to stay where they are, is it?" I ask.

Jack shakes his head. "We'll have to move them, change their identities. The Others have made it clear that they're happy to use your family against you now, so we can't give them the chance."

"It will be worse this time, won't it?" I guess. "This time, the Underground will change their looks, their lives. They'll be different people. Different enough that the Others can't find them."

Jack is silent for a moment, but then nods. "We thought before that not remembering you would be enough to keep them safe. Now, it's obvious that it's who they are that matters, not just what they know. This needs to happen, Celes. Though I don't know how my father plans on that when his memory fading machine went down in the rubble of Location Six."

It doesn't seem fair, doing that to them. Not again. "How many times are they going to have to uproot, Jack?

Is this going to have to happen every time the Others get close to them?"

Jack spreads his hands. "We're just trying to keep them safe, Celes. Sometimes that means doing things that aren't ideal, but it's better than getting them into the line of fire."

"Maybe, Jack." I don't much feel like agreeing with him, though. "Maybe it's just better for them to become *them* again, though. At least that way, they would know what they were facing, know why they're being put in danger. They wouldn't have to keep running the same way, and they could make their own decisions about what happens."

"That would put you in a lot of danger," Jack points out. "That would put *them* in a lot of danger. Changing their identities is the best way to prevent the kind of mistakes that would let people find them. Anyway, do you really think they would ever make the decision to go back to who they were, knowing Richard is right there, waiting to get to you?"

"I don't know," I admit, "But it is *their* decision, Jack. It's their lives, and they should be able to decide whether they want to take the risk or not. We shouldn't be the ones deciding this kind of thing for them."

"Then go and ask them," Jack suggests. "Talk to them."

"What?" I realize then that I've backed myself into a corner. If I'm serious about my family getting their memories back, then I need to talk to them, even though they don't remember me at the moment.

"You don't have to do much," Jack says, reaching out to put a hand on my arm. "Just find out what they might decide if they were given a choice. It will be more convincing if you know the answer before you speak to Sebastian."

He's right, of course. Sebastian will be more easily swayed by people who actually want their lives back than by some hypothetical situation. I force myself to head over into the next room, where my family are sitting, talking to one another with the kind of easy familiarity that families have. The kind of familiarity that I miss so much.

Bailey stands, going to get something from the corner of the room where the Faders have left out food, and I decide that's probably the easiest place to start. Not that any of this is easy. I move up next to him, taking a couple of sandwiches as an excuse to do it. Bailey looks up at me a little nervously, and I can see my mom and dad's eyes following me too. But then, they would. They just remember me as the girl who helped them out of the Fortress, after all. The strange one the Others claimed was their daughter.

"So, Bailey, what have you been up to for the last couple of months?" I ask, trying to keep my tone casual. I know I can't just walk back into his life, but I can at least ask the kind of thing that a friendly stranger might, can't I?

Bailey blushes. He actually blushes. "Ah..."

"Celestra," I say. "Celes for short. People close to me call me that."

"Just the usual stuff, I guess... Celes. Computers, comics, games. That kind of thing."

He sounds nervous, but then, seeing it from his point of view, he's a ten year old boy being asked questions by this girl he either doesn't know, or knows only from pictures half glimpsed in magazines. I try smiling to make this a bit easier on him. Though I don't know who is going to make it easier on me.

"That sounds like the kind of thing I used to do with my little brother. Play video games, talk comic books, stuff like that."

"You have a little brother?" Bailey asks.

Why did I have to say it? I have now, though, so I have to go through with it. "Yeah. He's roughly your age, a handful, too smart for his age, and gosh, I miss him." I move a bit closer to Bailey. "You remind me so much of him. Can I give you a hug?"

That probably sounds really odd, this complete stranger wanting to hug him. Bailey certainly seems startled enough by it. Yet he recovers well. "Sure, okay."

I hug him briefly, exactly the way I always used to. It's nice. Too nice, given that eventually I have to let go of him, pretend that there aren't any tears in my eyes, and make my way over to where my parents are sitting. I join them.

"Mr. and Mrs. Caine," I manage. "You have a remarkable and delightful son. Take very good care of him."

That pleases them, of course. They always like it when people praise Bailey.

"Thank you," my mother says. "And thank you for helping to get us out of that place."

"I'm just sorry they took you there," I say. "Especially over what was a huge mistake."

I know they won't believe me if I tell them that they're my parents, so what else can I call it? Even so, I see them staring at me.

"You know, you seem so familiar," my mother says. "Are you from around these parts?"

"I used to live not far from here," I reply.

"Thank you for saving us, Celestra," my father says, "but there's one thing I don't understand. "The man who took us and threatened us; he said we were your parents, that you were our daughter." His brow creases in that way it does when he's thinking hard about something. "We don't have a daughter, but something about that idea feels... it feels as though there is something missing."

Like his memory. Maybe if I push them in the right direction? "Maybe you had wanted a daughter, but couldn't..." I think of the footage of them getting me. "...couldn't have one?"

Does that trigger a hint of recognition? No, there's nothing. Not so much as a flicker.

"No," my mother says, "I can't remember ever wanting anything like that. Are you all right, dear?"

"I'm fine," I lie. "Just fine."

So anything based on remembering me is out. I just need to ask the question I came here to ask, and get out of this room before it breaks my heart.

"I... I need to ask you both a question. A hypothetical question, but I need you to both think very carefully before answering. Is that okay?"

My parents look at one another. It's my father who nods. "Sure."

"I want you to imagine your child, Bailey, was found to be remarkable. Not just clever, or gifted, or anything like that. I'm sure he's all of those things already. Truly remarkable. But I want you to imagine that would make it dangerous for you, and that there would be people hunting you. If it meant keeping Bailey safe, would you completely change your current life to protect him?"

"Of course we would," my father says. "What kind of a question is that?"

My mother nods her agreement. "We would do whatever it took to keep our child safe."

"What's this about?" my father asks. "Bailey isn't in any kind of danger, is he?"

I shake my head. "Bailey is fine," I say. "I promise. I can't really explain the rest of it to you. Not in a way that would make any sense. Just..." I reach forward to hug them both. "Thank you for being such good parents."

I leave quickly, desperate to get out of there before the tears I feel coming can overwhelm me. Jack is out there waiting for me, ready to take me into his arms. I let him, staying there pressed safely against him until I'm sure there are no more tears. It takes a while. Only then does Jack say anything.

"Did you get your answer, Celes?"

I nod. I have an answer, even if it isn't one that I would have thought anyone might have given.

"They would choose to be Faded to protect their child. They would do whatever it takes to keep their child safe."

"And they would want to keep you safe, Celes," Jack reassures me.

"They don't even remember me."

"Not consciously," Jack says, "but feelings? Feelings are harder. I've seen people who have been Faded completely, yet they still have the same feelings about other people they had before. They might not act on them, because they don't know why they have them, but they're there."

"You sound so certain."

"I am. It's not something we can explain. Feelings just seem to be stronger that way. But they linger. Time, space, even Fading can't change that. Your parents love you, Celes, and they want to do what's best for you."

I nod, wanting to tell Jack how grateful I am he talked me into asking them. How much I care. There isn't a chance though. Sebastian comes over, sweeping Jack away into some urgent Underground business or other, leaving me to feel simply grateful that I've had such a great family.

EIGHTEEN

When Jack goes off to talk to Sebastian, I'm left alone. I could go after them, but I guess there's a lot they need to talk about. I go outside instead, looking up into the cool night air, watching the stars. Is the place I came from out there somewhere? I walk out to the edge of the farm's fields, taking some time alone for the first time in days.

I've been looking up for several minutes when there's a tap on my shoulder. I look around to see Grayson offering me his jacket. It's one of his old ones. One I remember him wearing back when we were together. Given everything we've been through recently, I'm surprised it has survived.

"I thought you might need this, Celes. You look cold."

It's such a small gesture, but it brings back memories. Grayson was always giving me his jacket when it was cold, this jacket usually, and I used to love curling up in the warmth of it, with him close by. I used to feel safe. I used to feel like the world couldn't touch me. So much for that idea, I guess.

"Thank you." I take the jacket anyway and slip it on, because the night is starting to get cold, and because... well, just because. It occurs to me then that I haven't spoken to Grayson since the mission. "And thank you for getting my family out. I don't know if they would have gone with us if you hadn't been there."

Grayson looks a little uncomfortable with that, but then, he's never been much good with praise. "It's nothing, Celes."

I shake my head. "It's not nothing. You could have been killed, confronting your father like that. He could have decided to have you shot, or his men could have done it without asking."

Grayson shrugs. "He was going to kill innocent people," he says, as though it's what anyone would have done. But most people wouldn't. Just Grayson. "And your family were our neighbors. They're good people."

"People you helped to get out," I point out, "because you were the one they remembered."

"Yes." Grayson hesitates, and I get the feeling he's not sure whether to say what he's thinking. "*I remember things. Things about you, Celes.*"

I'm not sure what to say to that. "What do you mean?"

"I... I think I'm starting to remember."

"I didn't think that was possible," I say, because as far as I know, the only people who have shaken off the effects of Sebastian's machine have been me and Jack. And we're... well, we have the advantage of not being human. If you can call it an advantage.

Grayson looks straight at me. "It's all coming back to me, Celes. I remember... I remember us. I remember what we had, how close we were. I remember how we were going to go to the same college, and that I planned..."

"Yes?"

"I was going to propose to you when we finished college." Grayson looks away. "I'm sorry, I shouldn't have said anything."

My heart feels... I don't know what it feels like in that moment. "I'm glad you remember," I say, "but it's going to make things complicated. I'm with Jack."

"I know," Grayson says, but he doesn't *sound* like he knows it. "I know you've moved on to Jack, but I still care about you. I still remember that we never really resolved the things between us. I still remember this."

The kiss is sudden, catching me by surprise. Or am I kidding myself about that? It's so loving, so sweet, that I can't bring myself to step back, the way I know I should. It's Grayson who finally breaks the kiss.

"I will always be there for you," he promises, "no matter where you are. No matter what happens. I love you, Celes. I know you don't want to hear that, but I love you. I always will. Even when everyone else turns on you."

"Why would everyone else turn on me?" I demand.

Grayson looks down. "Celes, everyone here is happy to see you come into your powers at the moment, but there's talk. Talk about reining you in. Some of the Faders think you might be a problem in the future."

"The Faders?" I can't help being a little skeptical. "Is this about making me distrust Jack?"

Grayson shakes his head. "It's not Jack. It's not Sebastian or Jonas either."

I know who that leaves, of the key people here. "Lionel? But I... I *saved* him."

"And almost killed him, from what I hear," Grayson says softly.

I have to nod. There was a moment when I almost did it. When I almost reached out to touch him just because I could.

"He's grateful," Grayson says, "but he's scared too. And scared people do stupid things."

I kick the ground. This is so unfair. "I risked my life and Jack's to get him out, and he does this? I thought he was on my side."

"I think he is, up to a point," Grayson says. "It's just… people are scared of the kind of power you have, Celes."

"Are you?" It's not a fair question, but I remember he was scared back in the corn fields where my power first came out.

"No. Never."

"So, do Jack and Sebastian know what Lionel has been saying about me?" I ask.

Grayson shakes his head. "I don't think he intends for them to know, especially since he thinks Jack will do anything to prove him wrong."

"This is so..." I won't say unfair out loud, but we both know it's what I mean. "The Underground were *looking* for someone like me, with their whole search for life beyond Earth, and now..."

"And now they've seen what it means," Grayson says, "and they don't understand you, so they're being cautious. They're..."

Grayson stops, his head whipping around, just in time for someone to hit him with what looks like a short club. I turn and see Phillipa, the older Fader Grayson was flirting with on the plane over here. Please let this be about something as stupid as jealousy, I hope, but I know it's not going to be as simple as that.

"Now what you've made me do," the woman says. "You should know better than to rat out one of your fellow Faders, Grayson. Especially not the Major."

Grayson pulls himself back to his feet. "But he's going against what Dr. Cook wants."

"Sebastian isn't in a position to make good decisions at the moment. And he has been in the custody of the Others until recently. So the Major gets to give the orders, and his orders are to make sure that the girl doesn't get dangerous."

"Even if that means killing Celestra?"

Phillipa shrugs. "It's a moot point, dear. You shouldn't have told her what you did. You certainly shouldn't have let me hear that you've started remembering."

She moves forward quickly, swinging the club. Grayson steps inside the movement, trying to use his elbows to knock Phillipa back, but the trainer is expecting the move, hitting Grayson viciously with her knee, then following it up with a kick as the attack forces Grayson back. He partly blocks that, but it still knocks the wind out of him.

Phillipa swings her club in an arc that ends with Grayson's knee, and he goes down, crying out in pain with his leg twisted to an impossible angle. Grayson puts an arm up, trying to fend her off, and she breaks that with the club too. She moves down over him, pinning him with her legs while she raises the club.

"This is kind of a pity, Grayson, but we can't have you spreading tales. You or her. Just one thing, what are you? After all, no one keeps their memories unless..."

I've had enough. I throw myself forward, reaching down to touch the woman. The power in me is only too eager to rise up, leaping into her in a glowing blaze of power. She sits there for a moment, almost seeming to glow with power herself as my energy wells up inside her, burning its way through every cell, every atom. Then Phillipa disintegrates. As thoroughly and quickly as the Others back at the Fortress, Phillipa burns to nothing.

Of course, nothing can't support my weight.

I topple down, falling onto Grayson before I can stop myself, my hand still glowing with power. I try to will it back into me as I fall, but I'm too late, and I don't know how to stop it anyway. I touch Grayson, and the power jumps into him, heat rising up through him, his skin glowing with it, exactly the same as Phillipa's did.

I throw myself from Grayson, rolling to my knees with my hand over my mouth as the power subsides. "Grayson. No. Oh, please, no."

Grayson is so still. So still as he just stares up at the night sky. Energy still crackles over him, making him look like he has been hit by lightning, and I can't touch him. I don't dare.

"Grayson, can you hear me? Please, talk to me!" I hesitate, not wanting to leave his side, but knowing what I have to do. "I'll get help," I say. "I'll get Jack. Jack will know what to do."

I stand to go get him, but then I hear my name.

"Celes…" Grayson repeats, barely audible.

I rush to his side, bending to touch him despite my fears. I shouldn't do that though, it seems, because another jolt of energy leaps into him, making Grayson's back arc with pain.

"Oh, Grayson. I'm sorry. I'm so sorry."

Grayson sits up, facing me as he does it. His arm and his leg are still twisted horrifically from where Phillipa hit him. Only they don't stay that way for long. Grayson twists them back into place with a grunt of effort, and a second later it's like he was never injured. As for the spot on his face where Phillipa's first blow landed, there's no sign of any injury at all. It's like Grayson is putting himself back together piece by piece.

When he's done, Grayson stands, and he looks fine. Like there's nothing wrong. Like he hasn't just been beaten half to death. Like I didn't just nearly kill him with a touch. It's… no, I can't think of it as impossible, not with all the things I can do. Except that this is Grayson. Grayson is normal, isn't he?

I guess not.

Grayson looks over to me, grinning in a way that suggests he can't quite believe what has just happened either. It's kind of nice to know that I'm not the only one, though Grayson looks less like it's a total shock than just like something he wasn't sure about has just come good.

"So it worked," Grayson says.

NINETEEN

I can't help staring at Grayson. What he has just done is... incredible. And I'm saying that as someone who can burn people into a charred pile of ashes, like the one that sits where Phillipa was.

"Grayson, I don't know what happened, but you just put yourself back together like..." I struggle to come up with anything, but then it comes to me. "It reminds me of some of the toy figures my brother had, where you could just repair them whenever they got damaged."

Grayson smiles. "I know. It's kind of cool, isn't it?"

"You sound like you knew this was going to happen."

Grayson nods, but then pauses. "I... I guess you could say I knew, but I forgot. When I was still just a kid, I had dreams about being able to do this. At least, I guess they were dreams. This would have been before my mother married Richard. Before I even met you. I forgot about them, though. I don't know why I forgot about them."

The word "Fading" jumps into my head. I know Grayson must be thinking it too.

"But just now, when your power went into me, it's like it touched something in me. It woke it up. It's like I connected with you."

"Your eyes look normal," I say, remembering how Jack's eyes glowed after the moment when I brought out his powers.

"I feel normal," Grayson says. "Didn't you when you discovered you were something else?"

He has a point there. I know people wanted to make me feel like I was something special, or something frightening. And I was scared about what I might become, but Grayson is right.

"I felt like me," I say. "Me, just with a lot of things I didn't understand going on beneath the surface."

I look around, checking the area. There are no signs of other Faders, but then there wouldn't be. Most of them will be inside, recovering, while Lionel's group will still think that Phillipa is watching us. It means we have time.

Time to figure out what's going on with Grayson. Time to figure out what all of this means.

"We should tell Jack," I say. "He should know."

"Why?" Grayson demands, suddenly angry. "Why must Jack know? Does he know everything about you?" His eyes narrow. "Has he been everywhere with you? Do you share everything intimate with him?"

"Grayson!" That's not a question he should be asking, especially when I haven't. I just *haven't*. He has no right to go around asking me stupid, jealous questions like that. And why does he want to be so secretive about what has just happened? What does it matter if Jack finds out?

Except that I can't imagine Jack wanting Grayson to know exactly what he is.

"Sebastian and his team of scientists could help if they knew," I suggest.

Grayson grimaces, "Not when they think we're both dangerous to them. Which they will. Celes, that was a Fader you burned, not one of the Others. Lionel will be able to say that you're too dangerous."

As if to prove his point, the door to the farmhouse opens letting a group of Faders out into the night air. They look like Faders from Location Two, which means that they're almost certainly on Lionel's team. They look over at us, and I know they aren't just out there for no reason, even though they don't approach us.

"Maybe we could explain that Phillipa attacked us," I suggest to Grayson.

"Do you think they'd listen?" Grayson shoots back. "No one in the farmhouse would care."

"My family's in there," I point out. "So are Jack and Sebastian. If we just tell them what's going on, if we tell them what Lionel did, I'm sure people will listen."

"They won't," Grayson says. "Think about it, Celes. I'm the kid whose father is the leader of the Others. You're... well, they'll point to the pile of ashes here and suddenly they'll have all the proof they need that you're dangerous. Whereas Lionel is their friend. They've known him for years."

That sounds ominous. Grayson makes it sound like there's no way out of this for us. Like the whole Underground will be trying to kill us as surely as the Others, the moment we go back inside.

"So what can we do?" I ask.

"First, we deal with what's left of Phillipa. We scatter the remains and do our best to disguise the burn marks."

"And then?" I ask.

"And then we leave, Celes. We run while we can. We get away from the Underground and try to stay safe."

"Just like that?" I ask, hardly able to believe what Grayson is suggesting. "I can't just leave," I say. "I can't just run off and abandon everything."

"You can," Grayson points out. "You have."

I have. Of course I have. It's what I did when I was Faded. I left without getting to say goodbye to my family. Without getting to say goodbye to Grayson. But that just means I know exactly how much it hurts to do it. And there are some people I can't just leave behind.

"I have to tell Jack," I say.

Grayson shakes his head. "It's too dangerous."

"I *have* to, Grayson." I try to come up with a reason that will make sense to him. "Remember when I came to see you without telling him? How he followed me? How he thought it was a threat? And I have to tell him what's going on."

Grayson looks over to Lionel's Faders, still hanging around outside the farmhouse. What are they waiting for over there? A signal from Phillipa? If so, it isn't going to come.

"We can't go in," Grayson says. "We might not be able to get out again, Celes. It's too much of a risk."

"It's a risk," I agree, "but it's one I have to take. I can't just leave Jack hanging, and that's not just because of what I feel about him. It's about him and Sebastian. It's about my family. Jack can't do anything if he doesn't know what's happening."

"So what are you going to do?" Grayson demands. "Walk in there and announce that Lionel is trying to make the Underground into something it shouldn't be."

"You know I wouldn't do anything that risky, Grayson."

For a moment, he looks disbelieving in the darkness. "Do I? You were quick enough to take a risk when it came to getting Lionel back."

"And look where that got me." I take Grayson by the arms. "I'm not going to do anything stupid. I'm just going to quietly let Jack and Sebastian know that there is dissention in the Underground. Then we'll go from there."

Kailin Gow

"I still don't like this," Grayson says. "There's too of a much chance of Lionel's people stopping you from leaving. And we might never get another chance to get away from them. We might be stuck with them following you, regardless of how much we do to try to lose them."

"But it's a risk we have to take." I move away from him. Far enough that I can make a run for the farmhouse if I have to. "I'm going in there, Grayson."

Grayson doesn't look happy about it, but he nods. "Okay. We'll need to get rid of Lionel's Faders though."

"How are we going to do that?" I ask. It's not like we can just suggest to them that they might like to move out of the way, after all. And we certainly can't tell them the truth about what is going on.

"Just leave that part to me," Grayson says. "Phillipa's remains too. I'll deal with it. Hide them so that no one will guess what happened out here."

"So what do I do?" I ask.

"Exactly what they think you ought to do. Go back inside like nothing has happened. Like you just came out here to talk to me."

A minute ago, he was saying that was too dangerous, but I guess I should be grateful. Grayson has seen that my mind is made up, and he's willing to help me out with what I have in mind.

"And when I'm inside, I find Jack and tell him?" I ask.

Grayson shakes his head. "Whatever you do, don't discuss this in the middle of the farmhouse. We don't know who is on our side and who is on Lionel's, so we don't know how the people there would react if they overheard you. Besides, there's a good chance that he won't be far away from Lionel himself."

"So how am I meant to let Jack know if I can't tell him?" I ask.

"You persuade him to come out here," Grayson replies. "It shouldn't be hard. Just pretend that you want to spend some romantic time alone with him. People will believe that. Jack certainly will." Does Grayson sound bitter there? Somehow, I don't think that this is going to be all that easy, not if Grayson has his memories back. "Once you get him out here, we can talk to him."

"I just hope talking will be enough," I say.

Grayson starts to put a reassuring arm round me, but then seems to think better of it. "Jack might be able to help. He's the closest to Lionel of anybody, and Sebastian listens to him too. So either Jack will be able to get through to Lionel and persuade him that you aren't dangerous even after what has happened, or he and Sebastian will be able to persuade the Faders not to go along with Lionel."

"Didn't you just say that a lot of the Faders are more loyal to Lionel than Sebastian?" I point out.

Grayson shrugs. "It isn't perfect, Celes, but I can't give you perfect here. I've already told you what I think we should do."

"Run for the hills and forget about everyone else."

"Keep ourselves safe. It's not like Lionel has a reason to hurt Jack or your family, and I don't think he's an evil man. He wouldn't do It for the sake of It."

Maybe Grayson has a point. Maybe they would be safer without me there. Yet I can't bring myself to do that to Jack. I can't just run out on him, even if that's exactly what I did to Grayson. After all, I didn't get a choice, when it came to Grayson. And then there's the question of what Jack is. If Lionel ever finds out how much Jack's non-human half is coming through, won't that make him just as suspicious as he seems to be of me?

No, I have to go back in there. I have to pretend that everything is all right. That shouldn't be too hard, should it? After all, I've spent the last month or two pretending to be a completely different person. How hard can it be to just pretend that things are normal for five minutes?

TWENTY

Grayson moves over to the Faders between me and the door to the farmhouse, talking to them. While he does so, I go back inside. They don't try to stop me. But then, it's getting out that is potentially the hard part, not getting back in. I just have to hope that Grayson will be able to do everything that he's said he is going to. It seems like a lot to ask of him to hide the evidence of what I did to Phillipa, and get rid of the Faders who might try to stop us if we wanted to leave.

Do we want to leave? I won't know for sure until I've been able to talk to Jack. Grayson seems set on it, but it doesn't feel right somehow. Or maybe that is just the thought of having to leave Jack behind. I'm not sure I would be able to do that. I'm also not sure what the return of Grayson's memories will mean for the two of us. I'm with Jack, and I plan to stay with Jack, but Grayson being there makes things... complicated.

Jack isn't in the main room of the farmhouse, with the rest of the Faders. I ask after him, because I figure that anyone I ask will assume that I just want to be close to him, rather than that I need to get some kind of secret message to him, and a Fader tells me that he's in one of the rooms at the far end of the farmhouse.

I find it inside a couple of minutes. It has a door of the kind of toughened glass the Underground seems to like so much, letting me see inside to where Jack, Sebastian and Jonas are sitting around a table, examining a rock that looks a lot like the one we took from Switzerland. There are computer screens attached to the table, along with manipulating arms, and I guess that the whole arrangement must be some kind of scanner. Jack looks up and smiles, hitting a button to open the door.

"Ah, Celestra, there you are!" Jonas says beside him, as though I'm a guest of honor at a party, rather than a visitor to a secret base. "We were about to come get you. You need to see this."

As I get closer, I can see that the rock on the table definitely is the one from Switzerland. I wonder if Lionel knows that Jack brought it here yet. Given what happened outside, I kind of hope not. Images of the rock appear on the computer screens attached to the table, traced out in green lines and accompanied by a whole series of numbers that I don't have enough context to understand. I guess that they're some kind of information about it, but I don't know what.

Another screen shows a view of what seems to be crystals, but then I see that one of the arms poised over the rock has a microscope attachment, and I guess that the image must be an extreme close up of its surface.

"You look like you have been busy," I say. Secretly, I just want to get Jack out of there so that we can tell him what's going on, but I know I can't just blurt something like that out. Besides, if Jonas knows something about the rock we found, then I probably need to know.

"Oh, we've been busy," Jonas says. "Very busy. While you were out on the raid, I was able to get a lot of work done on it. This rock is an extraordinary find. I didn't think it would give up its secrets as quickly as it has, either."

That sounds intriguing, and for a moment I forget what I'm there for. I move over to Jack, and he steps behind me, wrapping his hands around my waist so that we're pressed close facing the other two. It feels perfect to be there like that. Like I've always been there. It's comfortable, but it's more than comfortable, because "comfortable" doesn't cover the kind of heat that there is between us. It's enough to make me want to turn and kiss him right there and then, even though his father and uncle are both there. I don't, but it takes an effort not to. And somehow I know that Jack is having exactly the same difficultly.

Thankfully, Jonas manages to distract me by pointing to one of the computer screens.

"Now, Celestra," he says, "you've probably already guessed from your time in Switzerland that this rock is from wherever you are."

I nod. That's why finding it was such a big deal, after all. And, given the way it reacted to me, I can't imagine it being from anywhere else. The rock and I are connected. The more we find out about it, the more we'll learn about me. I have to believe that.

"Well, it's certainly no ordinary rock." Jonas says, then pauses, as though something amusing has just occurred to him. "Although in one sense, the ordinariness of it is what is so extraordinary, if you take my meaning."

I look at him blankly.

- 190 -

"What I mean is that this rock definitely originated somewhere in our solar system. Our tests show a connection between it and our sun, so that the power it gives off increases in sunlight, while what we have been able to determine of its chemical structure suggests a near Earth origin."

"So it's not some kind of alien rock?" I ask. "And if not, what am I?"

"That's the question, isn't it?" Jonas asks with a faint smile. "All of the Underground's research has been based on the assumption of life far off in space, in other systems. Even other galaxies. This... well, taken with what we know of you, it's a little confusing."

I obviously look confused again, because he explains.

"What I mean is that this rock suggests that, whatever you are, you are from this star system."

"Okay," I say. "Um... unless I'm missing something, Earth is the only planet in the solar system with life on it, right?"

"As far as we know, yes," Jonas says.

"So that means?"

"It means you must be human!"

Human. I don't feel very human sometimes. Not when there's power rising up in me, and it seems so natural for me to hurt other people. And humans don't have the power to burn other humans alive.

"I can't be human," I say.

Behind me, I can feel Jack's surprise too. "Celes is right," he says. "Saying that we're human doesn't make any sense, Jonas."

Jonas laughs. "Oh, very special humans, obviously. Highly evolved ones, perhaps, who have moved a long way beyond people nowadays."

"Are you sure?" Sebastian asks.

"You've seen the analysis for yourself," Jonas points out.

Sebastian nods. "It's just... that's amazing."

Amazing is one word for it. Though to me, it seems more confusing than anything. After all, how can it be true? How can Jack and I somehow be more evolved than the next human? Even the idea of us being from another planet seems to make more sense than that, because at least with that, there's the idea of us having come from somewhere we don't know about. If we're from Earth... well, we know about Earth, don't we? And I'm pretty sure none of my science classes at school covered people able to do any of the things I do.

Jack seems to still be confused too. "How can we be human, Jonas? Are you sure you haven't just done the analysis wrong?"

"When have I ever gotten something like this wrong? Besides, I double checked. Everything about that rock says that it came from within this solar system. Now, I'm not going to say that there might not be civilizations on other planets in the solar system that we don't know about. It's possible that they could exist, and that they're somehow shielding their existence from us. Compared to some of the stuff we're having to deal with today, that's maybe not so farfetched."

"But you don't think it is that, do you?" I ask.

Jonas shakes his head. "No, I don't. I think that the Underground would have picked up more signs than we have if a civilization like that existed. And then there's the fact that you and Jack seem to exist within normal human ranges. You aren't conditioned to the kind of situations you would find closer to or further from the Sun. I think the idea that you're some kind of super-evolved human just fits better than that."

"But it brings us back to the question of how could that happen," Sebastian points out. "Unless you're suggesting..." He looks at Jonas for a while. "You are, aren't you?"

Jonas shrugs. "It fits."

"What are you talking about?" I demand. The last thing I want is two scientists going off into some kind of discussion that only they can understand, treating the whole thing like it's just some abstract problem for their amusement. It isn't. This is my life.

Jonas explains. "Barring sudden mutations, evolution takes a long time. Thousands, even millions of years. Now, we know you didn't advance to the point you're at on another planet, and there isn't much evidence for people like you in our planet's past, so that development has to have happened somewhere else, right?"

"I guess so," I say. "But where else is there? Where can that kind of change have been happening?"

"Nowhere," Jonas says.

"Nowhere?" Now, he isn't making sense.

"What I mean is that it can't *have been* happening, because the only place it could have happened, Earth, we would have known about it."

"So we're back to the start," I say.

"No. What if... what if instead of this having been happening, it hasn't happened yet?"

Jonas pauses to let those words sink in. I'm glad he does. There are some words that need a lot of work to accept. "You're talking about time travel," I say. "But that's impossible."

"Actually, there is nothing in physics that specifically forbids it," Sebastian puts in. "It's just that people have always assumed that the difficulties involved would make it impossible to achieve practically, while we have had to ask, if it is possible, where are all the people from the future?"

"And now we know," Jonas says.

I don't know if this feels better or worse than being told that I might be some kind of alien. I do know that I'm glad Jack has his arms around me at that moment.

"So let's be clear," I say, wanting to be certain about this. Wanting to leave absolutely no room for doubt. "You're saying that..."

"I'm saying that you are from the future, Celestra. As was Jack's mother. Very far in the future, because that's the only kind of timescale that makes any sense here."

TWENTY-ONE

What Jonas is saying seems incredible, but it makes a kind of sense, too. After all, how else can I explain what I am? What I can do? I stand there for several seconds, trying to let the idea that I might be from the future sink in. It raises as many questions as answers.

"If I'm from the future, and Jack's mother is, does that mean that we're connected? That we were somehow meant to find one another here?"

I look round at Jack, and I know he thinks it's true. It makes sense, doesn't it, that two people so rare, so different from anyone else, should find one another like this?

"We were meant to find each other here, Celes," he agrees. "I can feel it. Like we've lived a lifetime together, knowing each other, loving each other. Time can't separate us."

"That's very nice," Sebastian says, "but I think we should wait for a little more in the way of evidence before we start leaping to that kind of conclusion, don't you?"

Beside him, Jonas shakes his head. "Honestly, Sebastian, you have no poetry in your soul. Though I would like to think a little more about the mechanics involved. Think about it. We have proof here that time travel is not only theoretically possible but also practically achievable. So why shouldn't we be able to achieve it?"

"Because we don't have another few thousand years of technological and biological development?" Sebastian says.

"But we have a head start just in knowing that it's possible," Jonas argues, which sets the two off on a discussion of concepts that I can't even pretend to keep up with. After a minute or two of it, Jonas starts scribbling down mathematical symbols as he tries to make a point, and I turn my attention to Jack.

"We should get out of here," I say, and then remember what I'm meant to be doing there. "Maybe go outside together. Just you and me."

"Why?" Jack asks, his smile turning into a grin that's a long way from his usual boyish smile. It's a grin that promises a lot, all of it good. And sadly, it's not somewhere we can go right now, because there are more important things to deal with. Life and death things, if we don't get them right.

"Grayson is waiting for us out there." I keep my voice low. I trust Sebastian and Jonas more than the rest of them, but Grayson is right, we need to get Jack on our side before we tell anyone else. I don't have to worry too much about being overheard though, because Jonas and Sebastian are still busy debating the possibilities of time travel.

"Grayson?" Jack's smile has disappeared, to be replaced by a serious expression. He clearly knows that something is wrong. "What's going on, Celes?"

"I'm not sure I can say much here. Please, just come outside."

Jack looks at me for several seconds. "You aren't about to break up with me, are you?"

"What?" He thinks this is some kind of beginning to a break up speech? Okay, so I probably wouldn't want to do something like that in front of his father and uncle, but how can he think that?

"I know you were with Grayson before, but..."

"Didn't you hear me before when I said we were meant to be together?" I ask Jack. "I love you. This isn't about me breaking up with you, or anything like that."

"Then what?"

Will Jack go outside if I just ask him to trust me? I guess that he probably will. He knows me well enough that I'll have a good reason for it, but I owe him an explanation, don't I? And I'm pretty sure that, with just the four of us in the room, this is probably the most secure spot in the farmhouse. It's certainly the only spot where it's unlikely any of Lionel's Faders will overhear. I keep my voice low, barely above a whisper, just in case as I start to tell him.

"It's the other Faders," I tell Jack. "They're worried about me. They've seen what I can do, and now some of them think that I'm too dangerous to be left alone."

"Lionel," Jack guesses.

"You knew?" Would Jack know something like this and not tell me?

Jack shakes his head. "I didn't know for sure, but I saw what happened in the Fortress, remember. And at the start of this, he did express concerns."

"What kind of concerns?" I don't ask outright if he ever discussed maybe killing someone like me, but it seems that I don't have to.

"He was worried that if we found someone like you…" Jack hesitates, "like *us,* then we might not be able to contain the energy, and people might get hurt. He was worried that someone with this kind of ability might not have full control over it." Jack takes a breath. "It's a legitimate concern."

I know that better than anyone. I know what it feels like when the energy rises up in me. There's something wild about it. Uncontrollable. I know exactly how close I have come to burning people who weren't a threat, and exactly how hard I had to fight to push the energy back down again.

"I know all that, Jack, but it looks like Lionel has gone beyond expressing 'concerns'. He… he sent a Fader out to watch me and Grayson just now, and when Grayson tried to explain what was going on, the Fader tried to kill us."

"Who?" Jack asks.

"Does it make a difference?"

Jack shrugs. "It might tell me whether they were actually likely to have been obeying Lionel's instructions, or whether they were acting alone."

"Jack," I whisper, "it was Phillipa, from Location Two, and she actually told us that Lionel had ordered it."

Jack pales, but then, I guess it can't be easy for him to hear that a man he has looked up to, like Lionel, can order something like that.

"Did she hurt you?"

I shake my head. "She tried to kill Grayson first. I stopped her. I..."

Jack pulls me close, hugging me to him and stopping the next words. "Don't say anything about your abilities," he says. "I think Grayson might be right on this one. People can't know about it. I don't think it will be as bad as he thinks, but we can't take the chance." He thinks for a minute. "How is Grayson? Do we need to take out a medical kit?"

"He's fine," I say. "He was pretty badly hurt, but..." I can't not tell Jack this. "It was like he just kind of pulled himself back together. He repaired a couple of broken bones like it was nothing."

I give away Grayson's secret, just like that. I look down, not sure if I've done the right thing. How much trouble could this cause for Grayson, particularly given that Jack doesn't like him that much?

"Don't worry," Jack murmurs. "We'll help him too. We'll help him figure out what's going on with him. You said he was waiting outside, right?"

I nod, and pull on Jack's arm. "You have to come with me. He'll be waiting for us. We don't have any time to waste."

"It's okay, Celes," Jack says. "I'm coming."

We walk together through the farmhouse, and I try to make it look like we're going out for a romantic stroll, or something. Well, I guess that any Faders watching will guess "or something." After all, we spent more than a month living together. Still, if it means that they don't guess what we're really doing out there, I don't mind too much.

The moon is up when we get outside, throwing a pale light over the farmyard. This far from a town, it's a lot darker than I'm used to. I'm used to street lights, and curtains left open, neon signs and passing traffic. Out here, it's dark enough that I can't make out Grayson waiting for us. I can't see where Lionel's Faders are either. Has Grayson managed to deal with them for long enough that we can talk?

"Where is he, Celes?" Jack asks.

"I'm not sure," I reply, moving out into the center of the farmyard. Jack moves with me, looking around warily.

"I don't like this," he says. "Are you sure this is where you arranged to meet Grayson?"

"Yes, I'm sure. He was going to draw off Lionel's Faders, and then meet me back out here with you when..."

"Celes, look out!"

Jack moves towards me, reaching for his gun and trying to push me flat, obviously sensing something out in the dark with that uncanny knack he has for picking out danger. The trouble is, out here, so far from the farmhouse, so far from any kind of cover, there's not much even knowing that something is coming can do.

There's a soft puff of air somewhere out in the darkness, and something is sticking out of Jack's neck. It takes me a second to realize that it's a dart, like a zookeeper might use on some kind of big animal. I look around frantically, trying to work out where the shot came from and there's a second soft shot. Something stings my neck. I don't have to look down to know what it is.

"Jack," I start to say, but the word comes out wrong. I look around at Jack, and even that small movement makes my vision blur. Jack is there, but he's on his knees now, trying to point his gun out into the dark. Then I realize that I'm on my knees too. How did I end up like that?

Someone moves up to Jack, taking his gun from him almost gently. They slip a bag over his head as he starts to topple sideways to the floor, then another figure takes his feet and they lift him. I try to focus on them, but whatever is in my system is too potent for me to manage it. I start to collapse.

Strong hands catch me, holding me up. Part of me wants to thank whoever is doing it, but then I remember that I should probably be angry with them. I should probably be burning them. Except that I can't remember how to do it. I'm too tired. Too tired. Quickly, efficiently, someone slips a bag over my head too. I feel myself being lifted from the ground.

And then I'm too tired to do anything but sleep, so I drift into blissful unconsciousness.

EPILOGUE

I'm running. The sun is shining and I'm running. Not running from anything. Just running for the joy of it, through a meadow strewn with wild flowers, my strides eating up the ground. I'm running the way I have always wanted to run. Effortlessly, perfectly.

The place I'm running through is perfect too. There is a hedge along one side, from which birds dart occasionally, while to the other I can see fields stretching away. I run across the one I'm in without a care.

Then something changes, and I'm running faster. Not running for its own sake anymore. Running because I have to. Running because there is someone following me. I don't look back to see who, because I know, just know, that if I do I'll trip and fall, meaning that he'll catch up to me. I can't let him catch up to me.

"Celes!" he calls out. "Don't do this! Please don't do this. You may never make it back here if you go."

"I have to," I shout back. "Can't you see I have to? If I don't, then he will never come back either. I have to try."

I stop so suddenly that the person chasing me crashes into me, sending us both tumbling to the ground. I turn to look at him, but his face isn't clear. It's foggy, hard to see. It's like the sun is directly behind him. He looks down at me, and somehow I know that his expression is pleading, even though I can't see his expression.

"You love him that much?" he asks. I can hear the disappointment, the despair, in his words. I know he has hoped for more, but I can't give it to him. I can't.

"I'm sorry," I say. "I need to find him again. If I don't, he and I will cease to exist. We'll simply fade away. And..." I pause, wondering how much to say. "It's too dangerous for me here now. There are too many risks."

He gets up off me, turning away. "You know this could change the course of history? How much damage you could potentially do?"

"I know," I say. "Are you going to stop me?"

"I should. No one who has ever used the machine has come back. But I won't. I don't even know if I can."

I try to smile. "Promise me you won't worry too much?"

"Of course I'll worry," he says. "I took a bullet for you. I love you. How can I not worry? I will continue to love you. I will continue to protect you. Nothing can happen to you. Are you sure you have to do this?"

I nod. "I'm sure."

Celes, Jack, and Grayson's stories continues in

Forgotten (FADE #3)

Releases

March 2012

EXCERPT FROM

DESIRE

By Kailin Gow

****

Prologue

ᴥᵕᴥᵕᴥ

Arcadia, Earth – Year 3010

Perfection. That was how best to described the day. Blue skies with the hint of lilac and buttercream, fat fluffy white clouds gliding by, added to the beautiful day. It was the perfect way to end a sunny school day. With my hand nestled warmly in Liam's, I walked at his side, my face tilted up to the sun, my nostrils breathing in the fresh air that smelled like Spring lavenders and fresh linen. The fragrant air made me think of Spring formals, garden parties, and outdoor barbeques. The day could not be more enjoyable if it'd been planned that way. If I had not grown up anywhere else besides the state of Arcadia, I would have thought this was the way it always should be everywhere. I have lived in Arcadia for all my life, and have never known the skies to shine blue and clear otherwise. The only times Arcadia had ever experience dark skies and foul weather was rare indeed. This was just another typical day for a citizen of Arcadia. Perfect like the shiny spotless signpost on the corner of the street ahead was: Main Street, Arcadia.

School had gone well as usual, tests and exams had been passed with flying colors and the birds chip and chirp, whistling a merry tune. Like every day in Arcadia.

As we approached Nellie's Diner, I caught a glimpse of myself in a store window and was pleased with my appearance. My long blonde hair cascaded down my back, freshly brushed and tidy. The lustrous locks with a hint of lavender in them fluttered in the breeze in a way that always made Liam smile, and it all added a bounce to my step. I hardly fuss about my appearance, except to look presentable.

That morning I'd chosen to wear my pale green smock dress, the one that he always complimented me on.

"That dress sure does make those hazel eyes of yours pop," he'd always say.

I blushed. Always told I was a pretty girl, I never really believed it until Liam and I began dating in high school. At his side I felt beautiful. Was it his striking features that enhanced my sense of beauty or was it simply the look of adoration I saw in his eyes every time he looked at me that made me feel so beautiful? My mother, a single parent, once told me the most important thing about a man was the way he made you feel. Although there were other suitors besides Liam, he was the one who most made me feel good about myself.

"How'd you do on your math test?" he asked.

Though I'd always managed to get good grades, I never failed to get nervous and edgy when test time came around. "I think it went well," I said, smiling at him and adoring him all the more for the concern he always showed for me.

"I think I pretty much aced that History exam this morning," he said with pride.

He was so handsome, his fair curls so angelic. It never failed to amaze me how sweet, kind and generous he could be. A guy as handsome as Liam could easily break a thousand hearts, yet he was thoughtful and considerate in the way he treated every woman he met, and he was particularly attentive, loving and caring with me.

"Maybe my Life's Plan should have been to become a history professor," he added as he opened the door to the diner, his bright blue eyes twinkling with laughter and amusement.

I shared his hope and promise, and questioned what my own Life's Plan would be. With my 18th birthday quickly approaching, I would know all too soon. It was as though I had been waiting all my life to find out what my Life Plan would be. All of us under the age of 18 waited with anxiety and anticipation to find out what our Life's Plan held: our profession, who we would marry, where we would live, and how many children we would have. It would all be written in our Life's Plan.

"Kama! Liam," Sarah called from across the crowded diner. With her medium-length brown hair held back by a headband that matched her tangerine orange dress, she was easy to spot. "Hey, you love birds, over here."

We'd been voted the best-looking couple in school for two years, and some even said we were the most attractive couple in town. I couldn't count the number of eyes that watched us as we made our way to our table. I was used to standing out, having a natural tint of violet in my hair that came out when the sun highlighted it. It was the kind of color that salons had to mix a variety of colors to achieve. No one else in Arcadia, except for my mother had this, which made me stand out even more, right from childhood when I used to worry about looking different from everyone else. I used to cry about it when I was a little girl, why my hair was naturally different, and why people would stare so much. My mother would tell me that being different was good, and it was a good thing that I stood out.

As I grew older and less gawky, growing tall and slender with feminine curves, I began to enjoy being different, often taking the time to try out new styles. My mother said my newest style best suited me – long hair with bangs. Some of my classmates hinted at the added degree of elegant glamour my recently fashioned bangs gave me.

Others said it flattered my porcelain skin. I could only smile and nod. The attention we received was short of celebrities in a cozy state like Arcadia, and while I had always felt eyes on me, I've felt more scrutinized than ever before. After all, Liam was the son of the most important person here – the Founder and Governor of Arcadia, and Liam would one day become Governor, too.

It was all flattering, but it was also incredibly embarrassing. I felt watched all the time. Added to this was the expectation that Liam and I would soon marry. The thought both pleased and pressured me. I'd known Liam since I could remember, but the pressure to marry was sometimes difficult to swallow. Mother was around my age when she had me, but I still felt young and like a child. Was I mature enough, ready enough to get married and have a child within the next year or so? If my Life's Plan was to get married after graduation, then I wanted to do this on my own terms, not by everyone's expectations.

"After you." Liam gestured to the booth.

"Have you been waiting long?" I asked Sarah as I slid in.

"Just long enough to down one of these." She held up a tall, long glass of cherry soda then turned to Liam.

"You know, I was thinking, next week we could do the party down by the lake. It's gorgeous there."

"I'm famished. Have you ordered yet?"

"Two mini burgers with coleslaw and a mammoth burger with fries for Liam."

"Thanks," Liam said, obviously anticipating the great meal to come.

"So, what do you think?" Sarah asked him.

"I had thought about that, too. Streamers on the trees, flowers everywhere, and maybe even a live band? Or we could do something elegant and classy at my place. The grounds are beautiful this time of year with everything in bloom."

"I think she would really love that."

"I just love how you guys go about planning my birthday party as if I wasn't even there."

"It's as close to a surprise party as we can get. You always guess what we're up to anyway." Sarah pointed her straw at me for emphasis.

"But the night of my birthday is the same as the Arcades last game of the season."

"That's if they make it to the finals." Liam seemed unconcerned with the turn out of the evening.

"They always make it," Sarah added.

"Even if they do, everybody's going to want to come celebrate Kama's birthday."

It was just like Liam to be so optimistic. I suddenly thought of the secret wedding plans I had conjured up for us. As annoying as the pressure to marry could sometimes be, the thought that marrying Liam might not be in my Life's Plan often scared me to death.

"That's pushing it a bit, don't you think?" I knew I was popular at school, but for the student body to skip the Arcades' victory party for my 18th birthday was not likely to happen. Although I was well-liked, I was also from the Amethyst District, a middle-class neighborhood in Arcadia, and not in league with the most popular kids in school like Liam and Sarah.

"Look," Sarah said with finality. "The game is at two, will probably end before five, everyone will celebrate 'til seven and then they can all slide on over to our party for eight. Voila. It's all settled and everyone is happy."

My thoughts were drifting away from Sarah and the conversation. I tried to concentrate on what she was saying, but at that moment, I felt every sense in my body awaken to something I'd never felt before. It was electric, almost painful. A burning sensation that made my whole body tingled and buzz with intensity. Was this what closing in on my 18th birthday felt like?

No, it was more than just that. I stared out the window, looking for the source of my sudden distraction. The feeling intensified until the conversation between Sarah and Liam was completely blotted out and all that existed was that strong sensation as though I was being watched.

"Kama, did you hear what I said?"

I pulled my gaze away with difficulty and concentrated on Sarah who wove a lilac colored sheet of paper at me

I knew what it meant and instantly felt that jolt of envy. Having turned 18 a few weeks back, she'd finally received her Life's Plan.

"I finally got word from the Committee. Can you believe it? I hold in my hand my Life's Plan."

"And you managed to hold that bit of information back this long?" I said, teasing her.

"I love you and want this birthday to be special for you, but now that everything is practically settled, we can talk about *moi*."

"So, what does the future hold for *toi*?" I teased right back.

Before she could answer, the waitress arrived with our order.

"Everything looks delicious as usual. Thank you," Sarah said with a quick, polite but dismissive smile. She was eager to tell us about her Life's Plan, and it showed.

Beaming with pride, she pulled out her electronic pad, inserted the small chip she'd received from the Committee and turned the screen to Liam and me.

Ignoring the plate of hot food before me, I read through the introduction, though I basically knew it all. She came from the affluent Diamond Suburbs, was the only child to Mick and Fay Murray who both happened to work on the very Committee she'd just received notice from.

"Okay, so you guys already know that part," Sarah said as she guided the page further down. "Here's the interesting part."

I smiled as I envisioned the life that had been plotted out for her. She was to attend Arcadia University where she would meet her future husband in the Elite Society. Both would go on to work for the Committee and live in the Diamond Suburb.

"Oh, Sarah. I'm so excited for you." I finally picked up my little burger and sank my teeth into it.

"I knew you'd be. This is exactly what I wanted. Exactly what I was hoping for."

"Do you know how lucky you are to receive a Life's Plan that is just as you wanted it?"

"I know. I never would have thought."

I turned to Liam who'd sat silently through the exchange, his burger almost half gone. A wistful smile warmed his face as he looked at me. That look of love that came so often still warmed me just as much as it did on our very first date. He slid his hand around my waist and pulled me closer and I knew where his mind had wandered to; his own Life's Plan.

He was set to marry a girl he'd known all his life. It could hardly be anyone else but me. Everyone agreed we were the perfect match. He would someday take his father's place as Governor of Arcadia, but would start at the Committee. He, too, was slated to live in the luxurious suburb of Diamond.

How many times had he told me his Life's Plan had to include me? Countless. And every time he did, my heart raced a little faster. Life would indeed be perfect; a beautiful home in an exclusive neighborhood, a loving and gorgeous husband, and my best friend living nearby. What more could I hope for?

I couldn't resist leaning into him to snuggle. He wrapped his arms around me, kissed my forehead and chuckled in that soft way he had when he knew I was feeling amorous.

"Cool it, you guys," Sarah snapped. "I'm still here, in case you hadn't noticed. Besides, this is my Life's Plan we're happy about, remember? You'll have your chance in a few weeks, Kama."

Yes, I wanted to scream. And I hoped I wouldn't have to wait long. While some people waited weeks, as Sarah had, many received their Life's Plan within days of their 18th. No doubt mine would greatly resemble Sarah's and Liam's. We were basically cut from the same cloth, even if our childhoods were slightly different, but our destinies were bound to include one another.

The sensation returned again, drawing my attention away from the table and pulling me out of the diner like a magnet. I looked out the window, looking for the source of my distraction.

Across the street, simply standing there, tall, dark and strangely out of place, was a young man of such intensity, the hair on my arms rose. He was like no other man I'd ever seen, confident, sure and so attractive in his gloom. He was dressed like no one else in Arcadia, and his hair was longer, blowing wildly around his face.

While blue denim jeans were occasionally seen here and there, most young men of Arcadia wore stylish elegant slacks. But this intruder dared to wear not only jeans, but black jeans that seemed to have seen their share of battle. Instead of a shirt, he wore a dark leather tunic, bared at the chest that added to his mystique and aura of danger.

I was drawn to him in a way I'd never thought possible. It was magnetic. I felt my heart quicken and my pulse race. He was like a warrior straight out of those romantic fantasy novels I'd heard about. Extremely handsome, a bit exotic with his tan skin and jet-black hair. But his sapphire eyes held mine in a gaze that spoke lifetimes.

Kama, the desired one.

My fork stopped midway to my mouth. I froze as the strange and darkly mesmerizing voice entered my mind.

I glanced at Sarah. Happily chomping on her burger, she had not heard a thing.

Glancing sidelong at Liam, I could see he had not heard anything either.

I have found you, yet again…

Where was that voice coming from? I looked around and back to look at the mysterious stranger's face.

Him.

I forced the rest of my forkful of food into my mouth before the others noticed my sudden odd behavior, but I almost choked on it. When I finally managed to swallow it down, I turned to Liam.

"I think I just saw Tula across the street," I said as I laid down my fork and prepared to rise. "I owe her two dollars, so I'll run out to give it back to her."

He stood, and while he looked completely perplexed by my sudden need to leave the diner, he said nothing.

I hurried out and headed in the direction of the mysterious man with raven hair. Breathless before I even began to run across the street, I felt an urgent need to meet this man. But I could see before hitting the curb that he'd already disappeared.

My disappointment surprised me, as if I'd missed something important, something that could change my life. My heart felt heavy as I looked up and down the street. There was not even a trace of him until I arrived at the very spot I had seen him. Did I imagine him?

A perfect deep purple orchid laid on the ground where he had stood. It had to come from him. No orchid of such color grew in Arcadia. It was the only proof I was not completely going nuts. He had been here. I had seen him. I had felt his presence. This mysterious man with the burning blue eyes was here and knew my name. Who was he?

From Top Author for Young Adults

Kailin Gow

PULSE

17 year-old Kalina didn't know her boyfriend was a vampire until the night he died of a freak accident. She didn't know he came from a long line of vampires until the night she was visited by his half-brothers Jaegar and Stuart Greystone. There were a lot of secrets her boyfriend didn't tell her. Now she must discover them in order to keep alive. But having two half-brothers vampires around had just gotten interesting...

Kailin Gow

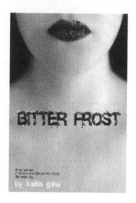

BITTER FROST

All her life, Breena had always dreamed about fairies as though she lived amongst them… beautiful fairies living amongst mortals and living in Feyland. In her dreams, he was always there – the breathtakingly handsome but dangerous Winter Prince, Kian, who is her intended. Then she sees Kian, who seems intent on finding her and carrying her off to Feyland. If she is his intended, why does he seem to hate her and want her dead? And her best friend

FALLING: FADE Book 2

Logan has suddenly become protective. Things are getting strange…

Kailin Gow

Want More Edgy books like *FADE*

Enter

the EDGE

theedgebooks.com

Where you will find edgy books for teens and young adults that would make your heart pound, your skin crawl, and leave you wanting more...

Feed Your Reading Addiction

Want to Know More about the *FADE Series*, Author Insight, Author Appearance, Contests and Giveaways?

Join the FADE Official Facebook Fan Page at:

http://www.facebook.com/KailinGowFadeSeries

Talk to Kailin Gow, the bestselling author of over 80 distinct books for all ages at:

http://kailingow.wordpress.com

and

on Twitter at: @kailingow

The FALLING for FADE New Release FALLING Contest

Win a $50 Amazon Gift Card!

Email a copy of your receipt of Falling (FADE #2) to:

promotions@theEDGEbooks.com

for your chance to win a $50 Amazon Gift Card.

Also, receive a FADE bookmark while supplies last.

This is an international contest open until Midnight December 15, 2011.

Winner announced December 18, 2011 on
http://kailingow.wordpress.com

No purchase necessary, if you wish to enter, send a postcard with your name, address, email address, age to:
Kailin Gow, 14252 Culver Dr. A732, Irvine, CA 92604

By providing us with your email address, you are agreeing to receive information about the contest, correspondence, and future contest announcements from theEDGEbooks.com, Kailin Gow, and theEDGEbooks partners.
Please allow 3 weeks to 12 weeks for prizes to be delivered.